SO-BIR-919

Vermont

SUNLIGHT
IN
VERMONT

SUNLIGHT IN VERMONT

•

VIRGINIA HART

AVALON BOOKS
THOMAS BOUREGY AND COMPANY, INC.
401 LAFAYETTE STREET
NEW YORK, NEW YORK 10003

© Copyright 1997 by Virginia Hart
Library of Congress Catalog Card Number 97-94270
ISBN 0-8034-9264-2

PRINTED IN THE UNITED STATES OF AMERICA
ON ACID-FREE PAPER
BY HADDON CRAFTSMEN, BLOOMSBURG, PENNSYLVANIA

SUNLIGHT
IN
VERMONT

Chapter One

"Can you drive a tractor?" Wyatt Rafferty looked up from the letter of introduction Gaby had presented to him and fastened serious gray-green eyes on her face.

She bit back the "Who, me?" that tickled the tip of her tongue and met his gaze directly. "Of course."

A tractor? What was she getting into? She shifted her position on the porch swing, inadvertently set it in motion, and almost dropped her handbag.

A section of the rambling blue-and-white frame farmhouse had surely been set aside for an office, with a desk and comfortable chairs. Then why was Mr. Rafferty conducting this interview on the front porch, leaning on one of the rails? Even though it was May—spring, even in Vermont—a chill nipped through the cable knit of her sweater and made her shiver.

For that matter, why was he interviewing her at all? Arrangements had been batted back and forth on the telephone between the Rafferty brothers and her great-uncle. She'd already been accepted—unfortunately—or she wouldn't be here.

Wyatt Rafferty was thirty-three or -four, she

guessed, the oldest of the three Rafferty brothers, judging by his in-charge manner. His molasses-brown hair, sun-streaked in places, might have been combed with a rake. But the dishevelment didn't detract from an appearance that under other circumstances would have been appealing.

His individual features—eyes, deep set, with a force behind them she couldn't read; straight, blunt nose; firm, show-me chin; brush of dark lashes, and even darker gash of eyebrows—made a pleasing whole. His forearms showed sleek strength, under rolled-up shirtsleeves.

He frowned and turned the page. "I don't see anything about experience on a farm. How did you learn?"

"I didn't. That is, I've never had an opportunity to drive one." She tried to sound confident. "It can't be so different from driving a car, can it?"

Had he simply cleared his throat? Or had what she'd heard been a snort of derision? "Have you ever milked a cow?"

Here was a question she'd anticipated. Rafferty Dairy Farms would naturally mean cows—lots of them—expecting to be milked, probably by her, according to the terms of her "incarceration." She'd seen miles of them on her way here, mostly black-and-white, milling around in neatly fenced pastures, or lying in clusters under trees.

"Isn't milking done mechanically these days?"

A smile played at the corners of his mouth. It was

a wide, generous mouth, unaccountably causing her to ponder what it might be like to be kissed by him, even given her frustrating predicament.

That possibility she would never explore, in spite of the three hundred and sixty-five days of boredom she faced. She'd made the decision to keep him at arm's length when she arrived, and accepted the tan, squarish hand he'd held out as she introduced herself. This went for any eligible male within shouting distance.

No way was she going to be caught up in a relationship—even a temporary one—with built-in geographical problems.

Florida-born and -bred, she was content with her home state. She loved not only the mild climate, but the relaxed lifestyle. She liked busy streets and lots of people. No man alive could tempt her into something that involved wrenching compromise.

It might have been foolish to contemplate that possibility at a first meeting, but experience had shown that the most unlikely people were drawn together, smitten before they knew it, and ended by trying to hammer the square pegs of their own personalities into triangular-shaped holes.

All this ran through her head in those first brief seconds when she'd stepped off the bus, and Wyatt Rafferty, whose rangy good looks were impossible to ignore, climbed out of his station wagon to greet her. Before she'd experienced the smug judgment in his manner that said he wouldn't want to get involved with her either.

"The pump still has to be primed." His lower lip slid forward in contemplation. "Milking takes the better part of two hours in the morning and two at night."

Four hours just for milking? When did these people find time to do anything else?

"I learn quickly," she managed.

"I see you have a degree in journalism, economics, and business management. None of that will be of any help." Obviously, he didn't want her here any more than she wanted to be here. So who had twisted his arm? "How about work experience?"

"I boxed groceries in a supermarket when I was in high school." She leaned forward to indicate the information in the folder she'd handed him. Couldn't he read? "It's all there. Since graduation, I've worked for Benson-Kessler."

"That's . . ."

"Mattresses. Sleep sets. Sofa beds."

"You worked in the office?"

"Yes." Did he think she loaded furniture into trucks or tested springs in showroom windows? "It was a huge office, and the work was varied. I ran computers, copiers, fax machines—everything."

Unimpressed, he twisted his mouth to one side. "Hmm."

It wasn't fair. She'd been on the brink of stepping into a retail analyst position on the day her great-uncle summoned her to his tower office and dropped the bomb.

When she'd agreed to work for Arnold Coburn in exchange for his financing her education, she'd expected her assigned job to be with Coburn Industries. Running errands. Filing. She didn't mind menial work at first. She'd done it at Benson-Kessler without complaint.

In her uncle's firm, while paying off her obligation, she was confident she'd have the opportunity to show she had the "right stuff." She knew she could contribute, especially in securities and investments—her forte.

But as Uncle Arnold said in his lecture, life wasn't fair. Because a dozen assorted nieces and nephews before her had let him down, expecting to slide by on his hard-earned money, he'd called a halt. Gaby would have to prove herself by spending a year working at Rafferty Farms. The owners, longtime friends, were shorthanded. After that, she and her uncle would discuss what happened next.

"You look exactly like your father." Uncle Arnold had studied her under beetlelike brows. "Let's hope that's where the resemblance ends."

"I don't know what you've heard," she began, needing to rise to her father's defense. "But—"

He cut her off in midsentence, a habit she was learning to expect. "Your father wasn't able to ensure the future of his children, was he? He walked out on his responsibilities without doing a lick of labor in his life.''

''He only wanted to—''

''I don't care what he wanted. I care about dedication. What about you?''

''I was in the top fourth of my class in—''

''I don't care what you accomplished sitting behind a desk.''

Gaby had been tempted to get up and leave. To make a speech first, of course, about how she'd pay back every cent he'd invested in her, as soon as she got a job. But there was her younger brother, Kip, to consider.

In three years, Kip would be ready for college. He'd need help, too. If she disappointed her uncle, he'd wash his hands of the whole family. She couldn't burn bridges for her brother.

So now she would begin ''paying the piper,'' as Uncle Arnold put it. She'd learn about hard work from the ground up. Then and only then would he consider finding a place for her in the family firm.

Thinking about it now, she could feel the heat crawling up her neck to her cheeks. She couldn't help being resentful, not only of her uncle, but of Wyatt Rafferty for his part in her entrapment.

He could have informed her uncle that he needed someone experienced. But no. He'd accepted the offer of Gaby's apprenticeship without hesitation. People willing to work twelve to fifteen hours a day for room, board, and pin money weren't easy to find.

Having probably expected Gaby, a city girl, to teeter in on four-inch heels, wearing an elaborate hairdo and full makeup, Mr. Rafferty no doubt felt a twinge of disappointment. How he would have enjoyed pontificating about what was suitable and what wasn't.

An eleventh-hour trip to the salon, however, had left her with a tousled cap of shiny ebony curls. Her long dark lashes provided a frame for her blue eyes without the help of mascara—not that it mattered out here, fifty miles from nowhere.

Nor would he able to criticize what she was wearing. Her shoes were ground-grippers, and her cotton shirt and pants had her geared to tackle anything. As for her physical makeup, she might not have been tall enough to meet his gaze at eye level, but she wasn't pint-sized. Having excelled in physical education classes in college, she was strong and agile.

"You were born and raised in Florida," he mused. *Deciding to attack from another angle,* she thought, anticipating his next question: "Ever seen snow?"

"It's that cold white stuff, isn't?" she couldn't resist asking.

"You'll see enough in the next year to recognize it. I doubt that you brought a coat warm enough to withstand a Vermont winter."

"That's where you're wrong. I came prepared." She indicated her suitcases. "Foul weather is better met with several layers of warmth. To be added as they're needed.''

''We'll see if that's still your attitude when an icy wind bites you on the . . . the back of the neck.'' The smile again, and though under other conditions she would have found it attractive, now it set her teeth on edge.

''Any questions?''

She had lots of questions. But she wasn't ready yet to hear the answers. ''If I think of some, I'll let you know.''

Briefly he held forth on the routine that would be hers as a Jack—or rather, Jill of all trades—including cooking and cleaning, bottling, scrubbing, and bread-baking. On and on. She'd be brewing up chocolate milk, too, and mixing twenty-four flavors of ice cream.

She could hardly wait.

''You'll be expected to pitch right in. We don't have room for slackers.''

She tensed at the word ''slackers,'' but kept nodding.

Wyatt looked unconvinced. ''Can you take hard work?''

''I've done my share.''

''Slaving over a hot computer?''

''Everything is done by computer these days.''

''Not quite everything,'' he said drolly.

She inhaled sharply. ''As you know, Mr. Rafferty—''

"Make that Wyatt. We move too fast here to bother with formality. In fact, there are a few dozen things I should be doing now."

Instead of wasting time with her? For someone who held forth on the principle of moving fast, he spoke slowly—almost with a drawl. Maybe he thought it was necessary to make her understand.

"As you must know," she tried again, "brain work can be more grueling than mere physical labor, and I've managed to deal with it."

His laugh was rich and deep. "You might change your mind about "mere" physical labor before you reach the end of your first day."

Across the road a piece of farm machinery on wheels sputtered and roared, drawing his attention. A boy of about fifteen, with the same mop of dark brownish hair, sat hunched over the monstrosity's levers and knobs. After making a few more deafening sounds, the thing lumbered into action.

"Watch it, Beau," Wyatt called in a booming voice that made Gaby jump. "That thing's been buckin' lately."

The boy raised a hand. "I got 'er licked."

Wyatt's grin made him look years younger. "Good enough."

Gaby swallowed hard. Would she be expected to climb into that seat and do whatever the boy was doing?

Her interrogator arrowed his attention back to her

face. "Make no mistake, Gaby," he said, picking up the thread of their conversation, "you'll need brains here, too. I hope you didn't leave them home with your swimming suit and suntan lotion."

"No," she said too sweetly. "As a matter of fact, I brought my suit too. It's only May. There are a few months before winter sets in, even in Vermont, aren't there? I assume there's a 'swimming hole?' "

"There is." A muscle twitched in his jaw. "I'm not sure you'll find the energy to use it."

"You might be surprised."

The smile faded from his eyes. "Well—we'll have to wait and see if you work out. I promised Arnold to give you a try."

Give her a try? Her toes curled inside her shoes. He made it sound as if he were doing her a favor. Did that mean—she hardly dared hope—that if her work was unsatisfactory, he'd send her packing?

On the other hand, if she failed, her uncle would find something equally unpleasant. If he had a friend who owned a salt mine, she'd end up there.

"I imagine you've heard the story about your great-uncle and my father being partners before Coburn Industries or Rafferty Farms came to be." Wyatt stooped down to scratch the neck of an aged setter who ambled over to rub against his leg.

"Yes, I have."

During that first meeting, Uncle Arnold had related the story of his life three times: from the moment he ran away at the age of ten, to his partnership with Cole Rafferty, the patriarch of the Rafferty family.

"Nobody gave me a handout," the old man had droned on. "When I stopped at a farmhouse for a meal, I had to chop wood for it and was grateful for the opportunity."

With effort, Gaby brushed away thoughts of that maddening meeting with her great-uncle, and its predetermined outcome. Stewing—or even kicking and screaming—would not help her now.

"My father fell in love with this part of the country at first sight. The deep quiet, the hills, and the change of seasons." Wyatt's voice was gentle as he spoke of his father. "When it was time to move on, he refused. The farm was a gold mine, he said. Arnold didn't agree. He missed city living and hated the cold. So they parted company."

The dog made a snuffling sound and settled down for a nap at Wyatt's feet.

"I heard about your father's death," Gaby said. "I'm sorry."

"His shoes have been hard to fill."

Cole Rafferty, felled unexpectedly by a massive stroke, had been gone less than a year. His absence was one of the reasons the farm was shorthanded. Then last month, Marianne, the wife of another Rafferty brother, Frank, had broken her leg and was temporarily confined to a wheelchair.

Hence, Gaby Holland to the rescue.

The machine across the road sputtered again as it cut a wide circle and headed away. A robin that had been perched on the limb of a red maple took off with a raucous cry. Gaby gazed after it, across a wide expanse of pasture to an apple orchard that was in blossom.

"Let's get one thing straight at the beginning." In an effort to be heard, Wyatt moved closer—so close she could smell soap, mixed with the scent of sunshine and hay.

"And that is?"

As he looked down, she couldn't see the green in his eyes—only the gray. "If we go to the trouble of breaking you in, you're obligated to stay the full year."

Here she couldn't make any promises. "You said 'if.' My uncle said it was all set."

"We can't keep somebody on who makes a habit of whimpering when things don't go her way."

"I don't whimper."

He pressed his lips together. "And I don't have patience with bellyachers."

"Bellyachers" was a word Uncle Arnold had used several times during their conversation when she'd tried to reason with him.

She tightened her fists in an effort to hold her temper. "While my uncle was discussing me, did he explain my reason for taking this job?"

"He said you did your best to weasel out of keeping the bargain you made."

Weasel?

The heat was creeping up her neck again. "I wasn't trying to weasel out of anything."

"Your uncle's words, not mine."

But he obviously agreed with the sentiment, and it wouldn't have done any good to explain the circumstances of that agreement to him.

Gaby's mother, widowed when Gaby was in high school, had barely been able to support herself and her family. The insurance money only covered pressing bills. She'd wept tears of relief when her father's wealthy brother offered to give her children the chance she wasn't able to provide. She and Gaby had signed the papers as directed by Arnold Coburn's lawyer, without reading them.

"When I accepted the terms my uncle set down for me, I assumed he meant something entirely different." She tried not to look as overwhelmed as she felt. Already she missed the warm sea air and the beaches back home.

"You expected to find your name on a door in gold letters."

"Not immediately." Actually, she did—and would, in time.

"That'll teach you to read the fine print." Wyatt's eyes, struck by a ray of sunlight through the trees, twinkled green again.

He actually thought it was funny.

Good, she wouldn't feel bad when Dennis found a

loophole in the unfair contract, and she could fly back where she'd come from.

Dennis Laird, a longtime friend, was an attorney and extremely resourceful. If anyone could find a way out, he could, and he'd promised to gnaw at it tooth and nail.

"If I'm free to take a decent job with a decent salary by the time Kip is ready for college," she'd explained to him, "I'll be able to provide all the help he needs without Arnold Coburn."

"Just hang in there," Dennis said as she boarded the Vermont-bound bus, feeling as if she were being shipped off to Devil's Island.

A year of my life lost, she couldn't stop thinking as the bus rolled along the highway. Spring, summer, fall, winter. But then it would be spring again.

On the plus side, Vermont was beautiful, with its majestic trees, its rolling green hills, and sweeping meadows. After all, somebody had liked it enough to write a song about it.

Evidently resigned to having an inept helper thrust upon him, Wyatt Rafferty unfolded to his full six-feet-and-then-some height. "Ready to see the layout? Or would you rather get settled in your room, and rest before supper?"

Rest, rest, rest, her senses screamed. Mostly she wanted time alone to think. But that was what Mr. Rafferty expected her to say.

"I'm not in the least tired." Resolutely, she rose,

too, and plucked up her handbag. "I was a passenger on the bus. Not the driver."

"True enough." He stepped back and waited while she swept past him down the steps with enthusiasm she didn't feel.

Chapter Two

"**B**eau." Wyatt cupped a hand to his mouth to make his voice carry across the yard, and the boy Gaby had seen earlier jumped off the tractor and trotted over.

He was almost as tall as Wyatt, and big-boned, with huge feet in heavy work shoes. His shaggy hair was covered with a baseball cap, set backward.

"Hi." He wiped a hand on the leg of his jeans before squeezing her hand enthusiastically.

"Want to carry Gaby's suitcases to her room?" Wyatt asked.

"Sure thing."

A restaurant, the first stop on the tour, was white clapboard with blue shutters and trim. The porch was blue, too, with ramps on either side. A window box overflowed with perky white flowers.

A sign like a theater marquee sat on stilts next to the road. It said: RAFFERTY FARMS—SANDWICHES, HOMEMADE SOUP, ICE CREAM, PIE, AND JUG MILK. The white-pebbled parking lot to the left of the entrance was empty, except for an RV.

"Where is everybody?" Gaby asked when they were inside. All the booths were empty. The floor had

16

been freshly mopped and a chugging from the kitchen sounded like a dishwasher.

"We're closed for repairs to one of the gas lines. But ordinarily we're only open till two anyway."

"I wouldn't think you'd make money with such short hours."

"We cater to the lunch trade. The few customers who'd stop at night aren't worth the manpower."

She hadn't known there was a restaurant on the premises. Suspicion washed over her and she saw the need to set the record straight. "I didn't sign on as a waitress or a cook," she said.

A subtle play of his features warned that he was annoyed. "You won't be doing either until I'm convinced you can handle people. Our customers are accustomed to friendly, efficient service."

"I'm probably better at public relations than you are," she said, joking in earnest.

"You may know that, but I don't." His squarish jaw squared still more. "You'll have to prove yourself. Meanwhile, I post a schedule every night, and we abide by it."

This was getting worse and worse. Besides milking and baby-sitting cows, she'd be wiping off tables and carrying trays? What other little surprises lurked in the corner, ready to pounce on her? Uncle Arnold must have been laughing himself silly.

"Surely it takes more than the family to run this operation."

"You're right." Wyatt nodded. "Especially with Beau in school. For seasonal work, we call on our neighbors, then return the favor when they need an extra hand or two."

"What do you do to fill in otherwise?"

"We have a few regular employees. Hector, who works in the kitchen, for instance, and Sophie, who's in charge of the restaurant." He considered Gaby through narrowed eyes. "You have something against waiting on tables?"

"I worked as a waitress when I was in college and swore I'd never do it again."

"Never say never," Wyatt remarked drolly. "We'll make sure you can handle it before we put you in a uniform."

Frustrated, she rolled her eyes ceilingward. "It isn't that it's so hard."

"It's beneath you?"

"Don't put words in my mouth." Now he was trying to make her feel like a snob. "I have great respect for people who can continue smiling while they balance three trays at a time, and keep orders in their heads, backing through a swinging door into a steamy kitchen. It's just that I'm not one of them."

"This isn't McDonald's, or anywhere close to it," he assured her gravely. "We believe in quality service, rather than quantity. When a customer wants his sandwich with mustard instead of mayonnaise, or pickle instead of tomato, he gets it."

Mentally, she searched for a stronger way of saying what needed saying. "You'll admit, won't you, that people who set their sights on one goal feel frustrated at being sidetracked?"

"Reaching a goal is seldom as immediate as any of us hope it'll be, Gaby." He rearranged the napkins in two of the dispensers on the counter. "Life is a board game. You go back to start if you land on the wrong space."

Was his moment of spouting philosophy the time to try to get through to him? "I took bookkeeping courses in college. Maybe I could devise a more efficient system than the one you're using and save you time and trouble."

His eyebrows pulled together in calculation.

She smiled, tasting victory. "Wouldn't it be self-defeating to train me for one thing when I already know another?"

"Are you finished?"

"I'm trying to tell you—"

"No. I'm telling *you*." He pointed his finger at her as if it were a .357 Magnum. "You'll do what I brought you here to do, whether that means being cook, maid, or bottle-washer. Take another look at your letter of agreement."

Her face prickled with outrage. "It didn't say anything about—"

"Don't give me a hard time, Gaby." He lowered his

chin to his chest. "It's noted that you don't relish your lot here. Make the best of it."

She wouldn't react. He was the monarch of this one-hundred-some-acre kingdom and he was welcome to it.

A calendar over the cash register showed a peaceful meadow, with black-and-white cows grazing contentedly. It was a picture that could have been snapped from the bus window anyplace in the surrounding hundred miles.

So why did these people want to come inside and look at the same thing they saw outside? Didn't they have enough imagination to expect a measure of the variety he mentioned—a vase of flowers or a Snoopy, for instance? Even the clockface was that of a cow, whose tail swung back and forth with each tick and whose eyes rolled, mocking her.

Eventually she and Mr. Rafferty were going to bump heads, but not on her first day—she hoped.

Someone was working in the kitchen. A young man with spiky orange hair and a wide grin raised a hand in hello, and she raised hers in return.

Wyatt nodded. "How's it going, Hector?"

"Can't complain."

"Gaby will be with us for a while. Give her all the help you can."

"Will do. How's it going, Gaby?"

"Fine, Hector."

"He's been with us for six years," Wyatt said as he held the door open for her to pass. "Listen to what he says, and you'll eventually pick up the kitchen routine.''

So he was still questioning her ability? In spite of her intentions, the words slipped out. ''I didn't apply for this job, Mr. Rafferty.''

''For the last time.'' He gave her a penetrating stare that said he was capable of pulling Excalibur out of the stone if he chose. ''You're here, and here you'll stay. Now. Shall we have a look at the rest of the layout?''

The bottling plant was a huge white building on the other side of the barn. Inside was a hum of machinery and a clinking of bottles moving on belts. When the bottles stopped, six at a time, spigots above filled them with milk, and they moved on.

After introducing two women—Bridget, a brunet in her mid-thirties, and June, a slim teenager who giggled her hello—he walked through each operation, explaining as if he were conducting a seminar for someone who cared.

''I thought dairies used plastic bottles,'' Gaby said.

''Plastic is more lightweight and makes for more efficient handling. But our customers are accustomed to glass and it'll take time to achieve a changeover.''

Ho hum, Gaby thought as he held forth about how the milk ran through a pipeline from cooler to cream separator.

"All in less than half a minute," June added, with a touch of pride.

"This is the two percent." Wyatt gestured. "The rest is reserved for half-and-half. When you're on duty, it'll be your job to see that the milk runs almost to the rim. Grab up the short fills. They have to be put through again."

"It looks simple." Gaby watched as the bottles rode past at a leisurely pace.

"Be sure and watch for overflows," June cautioned. "Or else we have to shut down for mopping."

"No problem."

"No problem?" Wyatt grunted. He took an arms-folded-across-chest stance. "Think you can handle it?"

Was he kidding? "Of course, I can handle it." *And read a book at the same time.*

"Bridget, you have a volunteer." His eyes glittered like gemstones. "Want to click off the machine until our newcomer's at her station?"

Gaby bit back a smile of triumph, welcoming the opportunity to show him up. The woman looked uneasy.

"It's okay," Wyatt assured her. "Give her a cap."

"This is precisely why I had my hair cut short," Gaby protested, waving the cap away.

"Hair-covering is policy," he said curtly, taking the cap from Bridget and plopping it unceremoniously on Gaby's head.

It fell crookedly over her left eye, and June giggled against her hand.

Feeling like Old Mother Hubbard, she adjusted the elasticized band so she could see, while the big boss went through the procedure again. ''Got it?''

''A six-year-old would have it by now,'' she said tightly.

He held up one hand, as if he were conductor of the Philharmonic. ''Let's give it a try.''

The first six bottles slid along the track easily and went on their way. The next six did the same, the next, and still the next. How many rounds would they have to make before Mr. Rafferty decided she had brains enough to pick bottles up and put them down?

Then unexpectedly, two bottles didn't fill to the top. Caught off guard, she still managed to pull them off easily. By that time though, the next set was on its way and two bottles overflowed under the spigot.

''Wait!'' she cried, grabbing at them and setting them right, but not soon enough to stop the next six bottles, and the next.

''Keep it moving.'' Wyatt waved at her. ''Grab the one with the broken handle.''

''Which?''

''Right in front of you. Get it before—too late. Put it to one side, so it can be replaced. Keep moving, Gaby.''

''I'm trying,'' she cried, reaching out barely in time

to arrange replacement bottles in their row. "Can't we slow the machine down?"

"The switch is already on 'slow.' "

Rescuing another short fill, she pressed it against her middle as she tried to catch an upcoming container with a broken lip, and to fill in the empty space. As she hunched forward, her hold loosened. The bottles slipped from her grasp, struck the side of the cabinet, and smashed to the floor.

"Cut the machine off," Wyatt directed.

Her clothes were spattered; so were the cabinets and aisles. In spite of her protective cap, she'd managed to get milk in her hair. When the conveyor belt stopped, she bent down to pick up the larger shards of glass. Immediately she cut her hand in two places, and blood dripped on her sweater.

"Harder than it looks?" Wyatt asked innocently.

"A little." She glanced around for something to sweep the pieces of bottle out of the way.

"We'd better wait till next time to show you how to stamp the expiration date on the cap," Bridget said. "It's tricky at first to avoid smearing the numbers."

"What do you use for that operation?" she muttered. "Your toes?"

Wyatt grasped her wrist and turned it over. "You've cut yourself."

"No kidding?"

"Sorry, Bridget," he said. "We'll get out of your way."

The woman smiled. ''No problem.''

''It looks easier when you're only watching,'' Gaby said, hoping to preempt a lecture.

''Doesn't everything?'' Still holding her wrist, he led her through another door. ''We'll get those cuts bandaged, then you'd better head in the house and change your clothes.''

''I have to clean up the mess I made.''

''I'll do it, honey.'' Bridget already had a long-handled mop in hand. ''Don't worry. This'll be second nature to you before long.''

Gaby smiled wryly. The thought was well meant, but not very comforting. ''At least I can put on my own bandage,'' she protested as Wyatt led her to a closet-sized room, pushed her into a straight-backed chair, and rifled through a jumbled medicine cabinet over the sink.

''Let me do it,'' she tried again, feeling an unwilling kindergartner being ministered to by the school nurse.

''Here we are.'' Either not hearing or not caring about her protests, he chose two bandages, pulled off the protective strips, and wound the adhesive bands in place.

Close as he stood, concentrating on his task, she was hyperconscious of a basic magnetism the man possessed. Maybe it was because he was more than moderately attractive by anyone's standards, and in spite of the antagonism that gripped her, she wasn't immune.

His mouth, so mobile as he expressed his expectations, was more generous when it was still. His hair, she decided, he kept moderately short, except in front, because of a tendency to curl if allowed to grow as it would.

None of this mattered. If he'd been a Michelangelo statue come to life, he was still her jailer, and from what she'd seen, was determined to make her aware of his lofty position.

"It should stop bleeding now." He studied his handiwork as he might have studied a tool he'd repaired. "When you've cleaned up, introduce yourself to Marianne and help her in the kitchen. I'll see you at the table. It's nearly time for lunch."

After what she'd been through, she doubted that her stomach could hold anything. "I'll skip lunch, if nobody minds."

He shifted his weight from one foot to the other. "Actually, I do mind."

"Good grief, why should you?"

"Because you aren't used to our weather or our rigid schedule. If you don't take care of yourself, you'll be a cinch to catch the first bug that comes along. Nobody here has time to nursemaid you."

"I'm in excellent health."

"And you're going to stay that way. At mealtime, you eat. I'm responsible for you."

Now she had a keeper. "Since when?"

"Since your Uncle Arnold put you in my charge. He

knows the pitfalls in the operation and he's concerned about your safety.''

''My uncle hardly knows me. We were lucky to get a Christmas card, probably signed by his secretary. I know when I'm hungry.''

''Did you argue with your supervisors every step of the way at this company where you were employed? If you did, it's no wonder they shipped you off.''

''They didn't ship me off.''

''Your uncle did.''

''Obviously you're misinformed, Mr. Rafferty. Uncle Arnold didn't . . .''

''Why do you find it so difficult to follow rules?'' His scowl was so deep, his eyebrows almost met with its intensity.

''Do you resent me for being a thinking person?'' She lifted her chin, matching him scowl for scowl, wanting to make it clear that she wasn't intimidated by his size or his bark.

''Not as long as you make an effort to fit in.''

''Why do I get the impression that you're in complete charge?'' She rose from her chair to trot after him. ''I understood it was a partnership. Isn't Frank the eldest son?'' Surely another of the brothers would be more reasonable.

''Frank's content to leave the operation to me. He's too easygoing. People take advantage of him.''

''No chance of that with you.''

''None whatsoever. Any more questions?''

"Not at the moment."

"Go then." He backed away. "I can't waste any more time with you."

"Waste time?" she muttered under her breath as she headed toward the house.

Spilled milk was beginning to dry on her ankles and pants legs, making her feel sticky. Beau was hunkered down at the corral, hammering a loose rail in place.

"Would anybody object to my taking a shower?" she asked. It wouldn't surprise her if she needed permission to take a deep breath.

The boy stopped hammering. "Dropped a bottle, did you?"

"A couple."

"You'll get the hang of it."

"As soon as I learn to juggle. Which is my room? I'd like to slip in quietly so I can look presentable when I meet your parents."

The boy pointed. "Yours is the second door to the left, as you go in the side door. Next to the bathroom."

"Thanks."

"Gaby."

"Yes?"

"I hope you don't have any favorite TV shows." He picked up the hammer again. "Our reception stinks."

TV was the least of her problems. "I watch a bit, but nothing I care about particularly."

"Good. The local shows are mostly old windbags.

Sitting around arguing with each other about how they're gonna fix the government.''

''We have shows like that where I come from, too,'' Gaby said.

''Yeah, but at least, you've got other choices.''

Someone was working in the kitchen and a radio was turned to an easy listening station. Water was running, and there was the clatter of utensils. The door was far enough along the corridor, though, that Gaby was able to make it to her room, then to the bathroom, without being seen.

Something smelled delicious enough to make her forget her lost appetite. Maybe she'd eat after all.

When she'd showered, she changed into a pair of navy cotton pants and a blue knit shirt with a boat neck. After she blow-dried her hair, she applied fresh lip gloss and dabbed powder lightly on her nose.

Beau had set her largest suitcase on the bed and the other on a vanity bench. She opened them, hung the hangables in the closet and put the foldables in three drawers that had been cleared out for her.

The wallpaper was yellow, with girls in wide pink skirts dancing around a Maypole. At least there were no cows in the scene. The curtains were dotted swiss and the floor was polished wood, with rag rugs thrown here and there. The bed was high and soft—a mite too soft—and covered with a crazy quilt. Another quilt in more subdued colors was folded on a cedar chest at the foot of the bed.

Like it or not, Gabrielle Holland, she informed her reflection, still somewhat of a stranger since her drastic haircut, *this is going to be your home for the next three hundred and sixty-five days. Accept it, and your lot will be easier.*

The room was cozy, but as she'd suspected when she'd said good-bye to her apartment, she needed something personal to make her feel settled.

At the first opportunity, she'd pick up a sheet of plywood to put under her mattress to add firmness. For now, the first addition to the decor was a calendar with a picture of a sailboat on warm Florida waters, and big squares that would allow her to mark off the days—a last-minute gift from Dennis, along with a black marking pen. Next came the vivid Salvador Dali poster he'd bought her at the bus station. This she taped to the closet door.

A framed photograph of her parents and brother went on the high-top maple dresser, along with snapshots of a mugging Dennis taken in a booth while they were waiting for the bus.

"Don't forget the good times," he'd written on the back of the strip.

As a final touch, she plopped her teddy bear, Mr. Troubles, on her pillow and stood back to study the effect. That was better.

Now she only had to clean off her milk-spattered shoes, plump up her composure, and go to meet the rest of the Raffertys. It couldn't be too bad. She'd already met the ogre of the clan.

Chapter Three

''Here comes the debutante,'' someone said in a stage whisper as Gaby picked her way down the hallway to the kitchen. ''I doubt she'll last the week. Let me call you later.''

Gaby considered doing an about-face and returning to her room. Since she was the only newcomer around, clearly she was the debutante. Why the insulting title, she couldn't comprehend, except it meant Marianne was another person who was less than enamored with her presence.

A woman in a wheelchair—Frank Rafferty's wife, Gaby presumed—was putting the receiver back on a wall telephone as she came in. About thirty-five, she had hazel eyes and a liberal scattering of freckles. She didn't wear any makeup, not even lipstick, and her sandy hair was slicked back and tied with a rubber band.

One of her legs was in a cast to the hip, and there was a wide bandage on her left wrist.

''I'm Gaby Holland. But I guess you know that.''

The woman didn't smile. ''You came in the house half an hour ago. I expected to see you before this.''

''I was unpacking.''

"Wyatt said you'd help after you washed up." It sounded like an accusation.

"I didn't realize. What can I do?"

"A number of things, before," the woman said tightly. "Now everything's been done."

Determined not to lose her temper, Gaby counted slowly to herself: *one, two, three.* "I'm sorry." Gaby pressed her lips together.

"I feel so clumsy in this thing. I get grumpy at times. You'll have to bear with me." The woman's words were apologetic, but the tone in which they were delivered was still resentful.

The kitchen was spotlessly clean, with red shutters over the window. Shelves on either side held herbs planted in metal coffee cans. A stuffed cow in a spotted dress sat in a narrow alcove. Another calendar, featuring—what else?—a cow, hung next to a wooden shopping list, with pegs marking purchases that needed to be made. Dish towels in assorted colors hung on a wooden rack next to the sink.

"We've had nothing but trouble with the help since my accident. A couple of weeks ago your uncle sent someone from the Houston office. He knew his way around a farm, but had allergies that made staying here impossible."

Allergies? Gaby mused. Too bad she hadn't thought of that. "I learn fast."

"But are you willing? That's more important."

"Not entirely." She might as well be honest. No

doubt Marianne knew the whole story of her contract with her uncle. "But I'm a good sport."

"We need someone experienced. Wyatt knows that."

"He agreed to take me on."

"Your uncle is very persuasive." Marianne reached over to open a cabinet on one side of the stove.

"Let me get that," Gaby offered.

"I'm not crippled," the woman snapped. "Yes, I guess I am. But I can do what's needed in the kitchen. Frank and Wyatt have been breaking their backs trying to do my chores as well as their own. Beau tries, too, but his mind is elsewhere."

"Like most boys his age."

"I know what it's like to be young," Marianne said, as if she felt called upon to defend herself. "But I grew up in a family where each member did a part of the whole job."

"So did I."

Marianne considered her, then wheeled over to turn off the radio. "If that's true, maybe things will work out after all. Would you go out on the porch and ring the dinner bell?"

The dinner bell wasn't a bell at all, but a triangle with a piece of iron like a drumstick attached to a chain. Gingerly, Gaby picked it up and struck iron to iron.

"You'll have to do better than that." Making a clucking sound with her tongue, Marianne wheeled out, almost running over Gaby's toe, took the hammer away, and struck the triangle on all three sides with gusto, until Beau waved both hands in response.

He was first at the table. Showing off for Gaby, he swung one leg over the top of the chair, toppled it, and had to set it right before taking his place. His face flushed to his ears.

A man Gaby assumed was Frank breezed in and offered a firm handshake. His hair, thickly waved and longish, was dark brown. His features were sharper than Wyatt's and not as appealingly placed. His movements were quicker, and his build more slight. Still there was an impressive resemblance between the brothers.

"Good to meet you, Gaby. I've heard a lot about you."

Considering who would have done the talking, it was easy to guess if it was good or bad. After he'd asked a few polite questions about her trip, the conversation moved to an ailing mowing machine, a broken coupler, then to a feed order whose bill had arrived that morning and was higher than expected. From there, it went to 'cruising fence,' on the agenda for the next week, and a problem with the silo.

Wyatt, who sat directly across from Gaby, glanced at her only briefly before reaching for a biscuit and joining in the exchange with a comment on how they were running a week and a half behind schedule. "We might as well be prepared to fall still further back before we're through."

Again his gaze fell on Gaby, emphasizing what they were all thinking. They would run late because they'd been saddled with a know-nothing city girl.

Not intending to be ignored, she waited for the first pause to ask about Marianne's accident.

"Sheer carelessness." The woman sprinkled pepper liberally in her bowl. I was in a hurry and not watching. I kicked the ladder away and fell off the roof."

What had the woman been doing on the roof? Gaby wondered silently, hoping that scampering over the shingles wouldn't be part of her job description.

"Lucky it wasn't a lot worse," Frank said.

"Don't let Mom fool you." Beau's eyes twinkled. "She did it on purpose to get out of the haying next week. She hates it more than anything else."

"You can say that again," Marianne acknowledged. "I'd rather dig ditches."

Gaby swallowed hard. If haying was unpleasant for a dyed-in-the-wool dairy farmer like Marianne, how would *she* take to it?

"Marianne's an acrobat." Wyatt aimed a crooked smile at Gaby, drawing an involuntary one from her. "She knows how to fall."

"I've had plenty of practice." Marianne took a sip of coffee. "Bad as it looks with this confounded wrapping, not being able to do what's needed is the hardest part."

"You do plenty." Frank reached over to pat her hand.

"Not enough."

"Around here, nothing's ever enough," Beau grunted.

Gaby stared into the depths of her bowl, not wanting Wyatt to read in her eyes how vigorously she agreed with his nephew's comment about the never-ending work ahead.

The stew was the best she'd ever tasted, and when a momentary silence allowed her a word, she said so. The biscuits were delicious, too, though they were re-heated ones, and the oven was an old-fashioned model that didn't look as if it would bake evenly.

When the meal was over, the men jumped up and grabbed their jackets, like firemen who'd heard the alarm. Beau bent over to retrieve the last biscuit and held it in his mouth while he wriggled his long arms into the sleeves of his windbreaker.

"I'll do the dishes," Gaby told Marianne. "Why don't you get some rest?"

"I can manage," the woman said, as if the offer had been Gaby's way of getting out of work. "You're needed in the milkroom."

In the milkroom, now? A flip-flopping began in Gaby's stomach. She was determined to prove her abilities. But not yet. "I didn't think anyone would want me to milk on my first day here."

"Any reason not to dig right in?" the woman asked. "There's hours of daylight left."

"I'd better change clothes then," Gaby said, hoping someone would stop her.

"Never mind," Wyatt said. "We've got enough to handle without a newcomer underfoot. Morning's soon enough to break you in."

Had it actually penetrated his thick skull that she'd just come off a long bus trip and could use a modicum of rest and relaxation?

She should have known better.

"You can still make yourself useful. Come outside," he directed. "I'll show you what to do."

She trailed him across the porch and down the steps, where he motioned toward a stretch of pasture across the road. That was Rafferty land, too?

"Might as well get a start on spring cleanup." He gestured again. "Work your way around the field."

"Work my way—how?"

"Pick up whatever's been dropped and forgotten, thrown out of passing cars, or blown by the wind. Wood. Tools. Trash. Whatever doesn't belong. Anything smaller than a cow gets overgrown by June."

"Rocks especially," Beau said. "They cause trouble if we run over 'em without knowing they're there."

"You'll find a wheelbarrow next to the house," Wyatt continued. "Your hands are small, but there should be some gloves that'll fit you on a hook inside the shed."

A wheelbarrow. More fun. She shaded her eyes with one hand. "How far does the section run?"

"To the creek in back, over the rise, and to the fence on both sides."

That was what she was afraid he'd say. "I doubt I can cover the whole thing today."

"You won't. Just don't miss anything, and remember where you left off when you start in next time."

"What about the house?" Through the trees she could see the peaked roof of a cottage. It had a vacant look. Maybe because there were no curtains on the windows and no path led to the door. "Does someone live there?"

"Never mind the house." Wyatt touched a hand to his nephew's shoulder. "Let's go, Beau."

"And if I have a question about where to put something?" she called.

"Ask Marianne."

"Ask Marianne," she mimicked under her breath, heading back to her room to change.

Five minutes later, she was suitably garbed for pasture-clearing, in charcoal sweat togs, and as ready as she'd ever be.

"Wait." Marianne beckoned for her to come back and handed her a basket. "Run down to the cellar first and get a dozen potatoes. You reach the door from the outside. Nobody ever got around to cutting access from here." Translated, that meant the house had been built by a man like Wyatt, who didn't give a hoot about saving the woman of the house extra steps.

The door to the cellar was built of weathered planks

nailed across several wider boards. The hinges squeaked in protest, and she had to use her shoulder as a prop while she struggled to attach the chain in the hope of keeping the door from crashing down on her head.

The stairs were steep and worn. A musty, damp smell tickled her nose and the air was chill, making her shiver, though her shirt was fleece-lined. All around were shelves holding mason jars of tomatoes, green beans, and a wide variety of other vegetables.

"I hope they don't expect me to do any canning," she grumbled under her breath.

Her grandmother had "put things up," too, and during the canning season, Gaby was called on to help. The kitchen would be like a steam room for days. The smell was overpowering as the woman stirred interminably and fixed jars in their water baths.

On the either side of one wall were bushel baskets with potatoes, apples, and onions. On the other were two steamer trunks. On top of one was a photo album. Curious, Gaby raised the cover. Inside was a studio wedding portrait. The groom strongly resembled Frank. The woman at his side was blond and very pretty. From the style of dress, Gaby guessed it had been taken in the fifties. Were these the elder Raffertys?

She removed the picture carefully to verify her assumption and saw that the names "Cole and Priscilla Rafferty" were scribbled in fine-tipped pen on the back, along with a date she couldn't read. So why were such important mementos kept in a damp cellar? She wouldn't ask.

Before she could turn another page, a knocking overhead was followed by Marianne's voice, asking if she'd found what she needed. In Rafferty language that meant, "Why are you taking so long?"

"I'll be right up." Gaby collected her potatoes and hurried upstairs, making sure the cellar door was secure.

Later, as she steered the wobbly wheelbarrow, ferreting out stones, rusty tin cans, and loose shingles, she hummed, trying to convince herself that Rafferty Farms wasn't so bad after all. She should have thought to bring a Walkman though, so she could listen to music. In fact, she'd buy one if she was ever allowed to venture into Woodbridge.

Before long, scattered moos hinted that the cows were getting restless. Feeling an ache in the small of her back, Gaby treated herself to a break and stood watching as Beau and another man she didn't know took charge of the animals' evening parade to the barn. Admittedly there was charm in the peaceful scene, with orange and red layers of sunset being edged out by blue and purple twilight—as long as someone else was doing the milking.

Sensing that she was being watched, she looked over her shoulder to see Wyatt in the clearing, axe in hand. At this distance she couldn't see his facial expression, but his body language was loud and clear.

Tote that barge. Lift that bail.

Glowering, she loosened a cabbage-sized rock that was much heavier than it looked and struggled to deposit it with the rest of the debris, trying not to appear as if she were struggling. The extra weight on one side made the wheelbarrow tip.

Though she ran with it, hoping to gain control, the wheel struck another half-buried stone, and the whole thing overturned, scattering what she'd collected for the past half hour all over the ground. Biting back a yowl of frustration, she stooped to put everything back, determined not to look in Wyatt's direction to see if he was laughing at her.

It was nearly dark by the time the moos tapered off, the milking was finished, and Marianne was battering the iron triangle to announce that it was time to eat again.

Another meal? was her first thought. Then to her surprise, she realized she actually was hungry.

Dinner was meat loaf, mashed potatoes without a single lump, and flavorful green beans. Again, conversation went over her head, and this time she was weary enough to allow it. Her friends always complained about up-the-organization types who couldn't talk about anything but their careers. Now Gaby knew farmers were no different. In another six months would she be spouting off about manure spreaders and the price of corn? What a revolting development that would be.

With dishes out of the way, she headed for her room to change for her nightly run. How many times had she dressed and undressed that day? It must have been a new record. But she was determined that at least part of her regular routine would continue.

Wyatt was stooping down beside a roofless tractor, attaching a gigantic garden rake. He stuck a screwdriver in his lineman-style belt and stood up. "Running away already?" he asked wryly as she started past.

"I do two miles every night at home." Trotting in place, she adjusted her elastic sweatband. "I don't see any reason why I should stop now."

His eyes crinkled with humor. "I know a reason or two."

"Exercise makes me feel better."

"You'll get plenty of exercise here."

"People think that," she said. "But they're wrong. The kind of work you do every day may be grueling, but it isn't aerobic."

"Aerobic," he echoed.

"It takes twenty minutes of continuous exercise for the benefit to kick in."

He came toward her, laid a hand on her shoulder, and all sensation skittered to that spot. Gentle as his touch felt, it held her in place. "Do me a favor and forget your aerobics tonight. Get a good night's sleep. I need you in shape in the morning."

"I'll be in better shape if I run."

"Humor me." His eyes were like jade in the near-darkness. "If you still feel like tearing up the road tomorrow, I promise not to say a word."

"Okay." Since he hadn't made it an order, she decided to give in—this time. She stopped running and took a deep breath. "Beau said the TV reception leaves a lot to be desired, and I'm not accustomed to going to bed early. Do you have any books I could read until I get sleepy?"

"You'll find plenty in the parlor."

Parlor? The expression sounded old-fashioned coming from him. "Thanks."

The parlor was large, and at the same time, cozy, with a hodgepodge of colors that followed no decorator's scheme and furniture in mixed styles. Plump couches with bright pillows, throw rugs in all designs, and inviting easy chairs would have made it a room designed to provide hospitality, if the family found time for parties or get-togethers.

As Wyatt had said, there was no shortage of books, but the selection wasn't great. Somebody in the family was interested in the fall of the Roman Empire. Somebody else in spelunking. Not tonight. She needed a stirring love story or an intriguing mystery to help her forget her plight. There were a good number of Zane Grey westerns, but for the most part the books were on new farming methods.

They even *read* about it?

After selecting a whodunit, she showered, put on pajamas and a kimono, in a lush shade of violet designed to raise her spirits, lay back on her too-soft bed, and prepared to be mystified until her body clock co-operated and she got sleepy.

"Settled in?" Wyatt asked, leaning with a hand against the door frame.

He'd changed to a wine-colored polo shirt that contrasted sharply with the rich tan of his skin. How heads would turn, she mused, if this man was a different sort and held down a job in an office. Admittedly, hers would have been one of them.

Why hadn't she closed the door? She knew why. There was no heater in her room and she needed the overflow from the furnace register in the hall to be comfortable. "I'm getting there."

"I see you brought all essentials with you." He indicated the teddy bear on her pillow. "A stuffed animal?"

"That's Mr. Troubles. I couldn't get along without him."

"He looks slightly worse for wear."

"He should. He's gone everywhere with me since I was six. Whenever things went wrong, or I was feeling sorry for myself, I'd hug him close, tell him my troubles."

"That's how he got his name?"

She nodded. "My father gave it to him."

"Your uncle said your father died when you were about Beau's age."

"Yes." She fought against the memory. "It was difficult."

Suddenly grim, Wyatt appeared to be struggling with his own pain. "The hardest part about loving someone is losing them."

Clearly it had been so with the loss of his father. How much more did he know about her background? she wondered.

"Dad was only forty-six when he suffered his heart attack, and in perfect health, we thought. It was so much worse, coming unexpectedly."

"No one's ever prepared for such a loss." Wyatt ventured into the room uninvited, to consider other changes she'd made, or maybe only to switch away from a subject that troubled him, too. "Is there a story behind this poster?" He indicated Salvador Dali's sagging clockface.

"Only that I like it." Not quite true. While she appreciated Dali's talent, she preferred his *Alice in Wonderland* lithographs. The stylized depiction of passing time had been Dennis's way of teasing her.

Wyatt studied the calendar next, cocking his head to one side. "White sands and sailboats. Your reminder of the land of perpetual sunshine?"

"It's a proven fact that we're emotionally affected by light. Light therapy is considered to be extremely effective."

"Light therapy," he repeated, humoring her.

"Don't laugh. It's true. Many people who are perfectly content in summer are hopelessly depressed in the winter.''

''And you're depending on the calendar picture to make you happy?''

''It isn't magic.''

His lower lip slid forward with what she might have thought was concern for her comfort, if she didn't know better. ''Is that what it would take to make you happy here, Gaby? Magic?''

It was a difficult question to answer without insulting his chosen lifestyle. ''We're all more content at home.''

''You lived with your mother and brother?''

So he knew about Kip. ''Not since college. I have an efficiency apartment. Only a pass-through between the living area and kitchen, and a couch that opens into a bed.''

''At least you won't feel cramped in these close quarters.''

''No,'' she admitted. Since he seemed more agreeable tonight than he had been earlier, she decided to take advantage of the occasion. ''I was wondering.''

''About what?'' He appeared to brace himself for another confrontation.

''Would anyone mind if I moved the bed, so the head is north and the foot south?'' It was something she'd read in a book about healthful living, and discovered that she preferred it.

He flashed her a ''what-now?'' look.

"It's east-west," she explained, gesturing to make her point.

"And north-south is better?"

"Something to do with the equator. Maybe it's all in my mind," she admitted, feeling giddy under his scrutiny. "But I actually do feel more rested in the morning when I sleep . . ."

"North-south."

Darn. He was even more appealing now than he'd been when they met. Why did he have to be so pig-headed?

On second thought, it was better this way.

"Do you care? If I move the bed, I mean."

"Not if it makes you more comfortable. Tell Beau after breakfast. He'll help." Wyatt paced off the proposed section of the floor, where the bed would be after it was moved, and nodded. "It won't keep you awake tonight, will it? Sleeping east-west, I mean?"

Was he making fun of her? "I don't think so." She had too many other things to ponder.

"Then I'll let you get to your reading." At the door he paused and cast a look at the stuffed bear. His eyes glistened with good humor in the lamplight. "Good luck, Mr. Troubles. No doubt, she'll be bending your ear tonight."

Chapter Four

Disoriented, Gaby woke to the lashing of rain at the window. Then reality flooded back and she groaned. For the first time since her final exams in college, she'd fallen asleep over a book.

Her feet were icy. She had a painful crick in her neck, too, from the too-thick pillow. With effort, she got up only long enough to wriggle out of her kimono and click off the lamp. Then she lay down again, pulled the extra quilt to her chin, and closed her eyes. Immediately she opened them. It sounded as if the house were coming down with the force of the weather.

Outside her window, the porch swing was testing its hinges. A shadow moved, and the noise stopped. Someone had secured the chain. Creeping out of bed, she peered through the curtains and saw Wyatt.

The storm had kept him from sleeping, too. Farmers had to worry about the weather. Not enough rain. Too much rain. His hair fell over his forehead in a becoming bracket, and his hands were plunged deep in the pockets of a scruffy bathrobe. Lightning flashed, and for a minute his expression was so intense he looked like Moses about to part the Red Sea.

The door creaked as Gaby opened it, but he didn't turn around.

"Need help building an ark?"

He didn't smile. "Why aren't you sleeping?"

"Why aren't you?" she countered.

"I've been going over the accounts, something I never enjoy. When I finish, I find myself lining up columns and adding numbers behind my eyelids."

She knew the feeling. "As I already said, I could work out an easier system and keep it in order for you."

"And as I already said, I post a schedule every day. You can help by following it."

She fought against impatience. Nobody was one-dimensional. Even this man had a good side. She'd glimpsed it in her room earlier. He looked younger out of his work clothes and even more appealing. In spite of his harsh words, he seemed approachable.

"Why do you change the schedule every day?" she asked. "Wouldn't it be simpler if everybody stuck with the same chores until it got to be automatic?"

"For one thing, it wouldn't be fair. Some jobs are more unpleasant than others."

Was he admitting that farm work could be unpleasant? "Makes sense."

"For another, alternating tasks makes for a more interesting day."

"Interesting" applied to dairy farming? An oxymoron, if she ever heard one. "Does it rain this hard often?"

"Often. We work around it."

She might have guessed that would be his answer. "I love rain," she said.

"Because you work in a cozy, warm office and can look outside at it."

"Till now." *Come on, Mr. Rafferty,* she coaxed silently. *There's a streak of humor somewhere in that lean, hard, dairy farmer's body.*

"Till now," he agreed.

"Back home we have a different kind of rain. Soft, warm, fragrant. I enjoy walking in it."

"Feel free." There it was. A small, but distracting grin.

She shook her head. "Ah—no thanks."

"Homesick already?"

Homesick wasn't the word. "Not really. An apartment is a place to live. Four walls. Tables and chairs. I've moved three times in the past six years, and a lot more than that when I was growing up."

Thunder boomed, lightning lit up the sky, and without thinking, she scooted against him. "That was close."

"Not as close as you think."

"It couldn't be, or my hair would be singed."

His laugh was a comforting rumble. "You miss your friends?"

"Some." She'd been working so hard getting her

degree, she hadn't had time for much camaraderie with anyone—except for Dennis, who was so emotionally tied to his work sometimes they were together for hours without saying anything.

"It's the uncertainty of a new experience, I suppose."

He nodded. "A person can tolerate a large degree of discomfort knowing it's temporary." Was he referring to her feelings, being far from home—or to his, and how glad he'd be to see the last of her?

"You're shivering." He closed his fingers around her upper arm, unaccountably making her shiver still more. "Better get inside."

"I can't sleep." She looked toward the driveway, where rain was rushing, forming a creek that threatened to carry the pickup truck away.

"You'll wish you had in the morning." He studied her, his expression enigmatic. "What about your book? Have you decided who the murderer is?"

"Not yet." How had he guessed that she was reading a mystery? She didn't say that she'd scanned only a few pages. It might lead him to suspect that she'd been too occupied with her own thoughts, mostly about breaking through the brick wall of his attitude, to concentrate on much else.

The night had mellowed him, and though he'd left a door open for her to explain about her dashed ambitions, she decided against it. He'd accuse her of "bellyaching" again. Instead, she joined him in gazing quietly at the swaying shapes of the trees, like threatening demons in the night.

"You need your sleep," he tried again, his persistence ruffling her feathers. Did he want so much to be alone, or was he only uncomfortable in her presence?

"Don't you need yours?"

"You turn everything I say back at me," he muttered. "It's irritating."

"My guess is that my presence within a fifty-mile radius irritates you."

"If I didn't need you," he shot back, "you wouldn't be here."

"I assumed you were doing Uncle Arnold a favor."

He shifted his stance to face her. "We need workers, inept or not."

"I'm not inept."

"We'll soon see, won't we?"

The arctic silence of their unspoken thoughts merged with the storm. Thunder crashed again, and lightning illuminated his face. His features twisted briefly, softened, then twisted again. For a moment she wondered if he would tear a page from Hamlet's book, point a finger at the door, and bellow for her to begone.

Instead, he grasped the silk lapels of her kimono and drew her toward him. Her heartbeat sounded in her ears, louder than the rain. Something akin to an out-of-body experience caught her up, and she sucked in her breath.

"Gaby," he said quietly, then stopped, as if her name was all he'd meant to say.

Adjusting his hold to grasp flesh and bone instead of fabric, he pulled her still closer and slanted his mouth over hers, warm and pleasurable. Like no kiss she'd ever known, it caught up her equilibrium, shook it, and turned it inside out, until she hadn't a logical thought in her head.

By the time he released her, she was left with lips that throbbed for more, and a sweet ache in her middle. Tilting her head back, she focused on his face. Though his expression said he planned to kiss her again, he didn't.

"If that's your idea of a 'Welcome to Rafferty Farms,' " she managed, knowing how ragged her voice sounded, "it's late in coming."

"I thought if you're accustomed to that sort of good night, a kiss might send you to your bed," he said darkly.

All was silent again, even the humming in her heart. The rain stopped abruptly, as if he had power over the forces of nature, too.

He'd kissed her because he assumed it was what she wanted? He supposed she'd joined him on the porch because she wanted his attentions? Not bothering to deny his insulting comment, she walked, rubber-limbed, into the house and let the screen door slap behind her.

Her reaction to his kiss was to be expected, she

mused as she lay in bed trying not to feel foolish. For the last two years, her dates with Dennis had been perfunctory. Here was an attractive, unattached man, however impossible, and the inevitable happened.

Going over the crushing things she should have said and would have, if she hadn't been knocked off balance, she fought the impulse to watch his movements through the thinly curtained window.

Not until she heard him come inside, and his footsteps moved to the end of the hall, did she close her eyes and sleep.

Mr. Troubles was in her dream. He was giant-sized, though. Unlike his normal self, when she called to him, he turned away. Then he was gone and she was waiting at a bus stop. The trees around her were menacing, like those in *Snow White,* and the rain was falling in sheets, causing bitterly cold water to rise around her ankles.

The bus arrived. But it didn't stop. She ran after it and pounded on the door, but the people inside only laughed.

"Let me in," she cried. "Please. Let me in."

The hammering continued, even after she opened her eyes. It was chilly and shadowy, and she was in a strange room. She sat up with a start, clutching the tangled quilt as the door flew open and light flooded across her bed.

Wyatt filled the opening. "Didn't you hear me calling?"

Her eyelids felt glued together. "What's wrong?"

"Did you expect to lie in bed all day?"

"At least until the sun came up." She flopped back again and threw an arm over her eyes.

"Not anymore. Get up." In three strides he crossed the room and forced her to her feet.

What was the use in arguing?

"You'll be getting up with the chickens," Dennis had warned, flapping his arms and doing a comical "cock-a-doodle-doo."

"I'll be okay after I have something warm in my stomach," she moaned, sitting down.

Again Wyatt pulled her to a standing position. "We don't eat until after the milking. The cows come first."

"Why should they care when they're milked?"

"They do. Take my word for it."

The floor was icy, making her step groggily to her bedside rug. "Don't you leave the heat on at night?"

"We keep the thermostat on low."

"Low meaning—zero?"

"If I let you go, can you stand up?"

She nodded and yanked herself free.

"I'll check back in five minutes." He stopped with a hand on the door, ready to say more.

"Go away." Groaning, she stumbled to the door and closed it. Off came her pajama top. She replaced it with a T-shirt, then a fleece sweatshirt with a hood. Forgetting her pajama pants, she almost pulled her jeans over them. Then came her socks and shoes.

As she staggered into the kitchen, Frank handed her a steaming cup. ''Coffee, Sunshine.''

''I'd rather have tea.'' If ''Sunshine'' was the nickname he'd chosen for her it was ludicrously ill-fitting.

''Camomile or orange pekoe?'' Wyatt asked solicitously.

''Either,'' she said numbly, then blinked when the others laughed.

''We don't have any tea,'' he said. ''Nobody here drinks it.''

''You make tea drinking sound like one of the seven deadly sins.''

''It is,'' Beau assured her. ''I couldn't make my way out the door without my coffee. Sure you don't want some?''

She rubbed her arms vigorously, trying to start the circulation. ''My parents never introduced it to me, so I never developed a taste.''

''Then you're finished,'' Wyatt said, starting her on her way outside.

The rain had stopped, but the ground was full of standing puddles. She tried to hop one but only succeeded in splashing freezing water on her ankles. Frank and Beau trotted one way to gather the cows, while she and Wyatt headed for the milking shed.

''That's Cleo,'' Wyatt said as one cow, smaller than the others, with a star pattern on her forehead, rushed ahead to find the place she wanted.

''They all have names?'' she marveled.

"A few make themselves known. Cleo was a runt. Nobody thought she'd make it. There you go, girl. That's it. This one is Dilly. She's the clown of the lot."

Gaby watched while he fastened one cow in place, then another, with a contraption made up of pipes shaped like halters.

"I'll just watch this morning," Gaby suggested, guessing that even the cows knew she hadn't the faintest idea of what she was doing.

"No time for spectators. I'll work this side, and you work the other."

Accepting her lot, she set about guiding other animals into their places. It was only a matter of allowing them to do what they would have done anyhow, she decided. Ropes had been hooked across the width of the door to keep the second shift of animals back until the first were through.

Her fingers felt stiff with cold as she followed suit, speaking in the same soothing tones Wyatt used. It was the middle of May. Wasn't there such a thing as spring in Vermont?

As she positioned her first cow and started for the second, her foot hit a protruding board and she stumbled. Startled by her movement, the cow emitted a loud moo and reared back.

"No, no, girl." Dread throbbed in her temples. "You belong in here. Please."

Snorting, the animal hurled itself to one side with such force, Gaby was thrown against the wall. In attempting to right herself she brought up one hand, hit it on a metal bar, and sat down hard.

"You plan to sit on the floor while I do the work?" Wyatt bounded over the barrier to snatch up a handful of her sweatshirt and pull her away as the cow reared again. "That animal weighs about seven hundred pounds."

"You think I'm sitting down because I want to take a rest?"

"I don't know what you're doing." His gaze swept from her forehead to her ankles. "Are you hurt?"

"No," she said, even though her hand was throbbing and already beginning to swell.

Confused, the cow galloped past her into the yard, followed by a shouting Beau.

"Catch her," Frank called, settling the remaining animals down with effort.

"Here she comes," Beau answered. "Oh, oh. There she goes."

"Wyatt," Frank said, joining the chase. "Take over."

Wyatt shifted into his brother's position. "Gaby, get the others in position. This time secure the stanchion."

Minutes later, Beau was back, leading the errant cow, now docile, on a rope. "She's okay. She was just scared."

"*She* was scared?" Gaby questioned.

"Cows booger easy, like bulls," Beau told her.

"That's why old-time cowboys sang to their animals, to keep 'em from stampeding."

"What kind of music do they prefer?" Gaby turned from the last animal, the click assuring her that she'd done it right this time. "Rock or classical?"

"Anything but a female shrieking," Wyatt grunted.

"I didn't shriek."

"Cover that side, Beau," he directed. "I'll get Gaby started over here."

Feeling thoroughly rebuked, she shook her head. "I suppose you were born knowing how to do this."

"No, but I watched and learned." Wyatt thrust out a warning hand. "That one's getting away from you."

"No, she's not." Gaby tried to sound confident as she fingered the bent piping. "I'd like to see you try to work in front of a computer screen."

"I'm as familiar with computers as I need to be. But if signed on to handle an advanced program, I'd do it."

"And I'll do this."

"You're right about that. We figure two minutes to secure. Three, tops. Then we move on."

"I didn't know it was such an art," she snapped.

His jaw squared. "Keep your eyes on what you're doing and forget the wisecracks."

Slowly and carefully for her benefit, he positioned himself and waited for her to nod her understanding at each explanation. First he spritzed disinfectant on the animal's udders. Then he began a steady, methodical stroking.

"Firm, but gentle," he recited. "Firm, but gentle." After he'd coaxed out a stream of milk, he slipped on suction cups with hoses attached to hooks on the ceiling. "It should take eight minutes or less for each cow."

"Two minutes. Eight minutes." She pictured the slow shuffle and easy drawl of actors who played farmers in the movies. "Why set time limits?"

Not answering, he stepped back. "Try it."

The cow's soft brown eyes studied Gaby's as if the animal knew she hadn't the slightest idea of how to begin. Struggling with an unspoken protest, she sank onto the stool Wyatt had vacated and followed each step he'd shown her.

"Firm, but gentle," she muttered. Nothing happened. "It doesn't work."

From his side of the aisle, Beau snickered.

"It works." Again Wyatt showed her, finishing up the first batch alone until Frank sent the next in.

The second time she was no more successful, but on the third round, she actually got milk.

"Yes, yes, yes." She made fists of her hands and shook them in the air.

Wyatt bit back a smile, as if he begrudged allowing her to see it. "If you've got it, I'll handle the other side and let Beau get back to his own chores."

"I've got it."

"By George, she's got it," Frank said, mimicking Professor Higgins's elation over Eliza Doolittle's performance in *My Fair Lady*.

"By George, she's got it," Beau echoed, and the two went into an off-key chorus of "The Rain in Spain."

From somewhere far off, a rooster crowed, and another joined in as she and Frank left the milking shed nearly two hours later. "They're complaining," she grunted, "because we woke them up."

"They depend on us to shake them off their nests."

"I wouldn't doubt it."

"You did good, Sunshine."

"Humph. Now I know how to milk a cow. I can hardly wait to add that to my résumé."

He ruffled her hair good-naturedly. "'Count each day lost you haven't learned something,' somebody said."

"It wasn't me," she assured him.

"You'll feel better after a big breakfast." He held the door open and waited for her to go into the kitchen first.

The morning's furor had driven away her appetite. "I usually just have soup in the morning."

"Soup?" He twisted his face comically.

"I open a can, heat it, and I'm on my way. One-two-three. My cabinet is filled with fifty-seven varieties. Chicken noodle, tomato, cream of mushroom. Whatever tickles my fancy."

"No soup here," Marianne, overhearing, told her in a flat tone.

"I'm not much for cereal." Gaby slipped out of her sweater and hung it on a peg with the others. The thought of oatmeal, gray and thick in the waiting pan, made her stomach lurch.

"No eggs or bacon?" Beau asked.

All that cholesterol? Gaby didn't say. "I'm not hungry enough for a heavy meal."

"This isn't a restaurant." Wyatt took his place at the table and patted the seat beside him. "Sit. You'll learn to eat what's here without complaining."

"I'm not complaining."

"You could have fooled me."

"I love this," Marianne snapped. "I work over a hot stove fixing an appetizing meal and you two make it sound like punishment."

"It's only that I . . ." Gaby abandoned her explanation as useless. "Do you have any milk?"

Laughing, Beau choked on his coffee. "Hey, guys, do *we* have milk?"

"Maybe we can locate a few gallons," Wyatt said dryly.

"Fine. I'll have a glass. And one of those popovers. They smell wonderful."

"That's all you're having?" Beau marveled.

Wyatt shrugged and turned his attention to his own plate. "Don't complain that you're hungry later."

As if she would. With the meal over, all she wanted

to do after a brisk, steaming-hot, fifteen-minute shower, was to stretch out on the bed and make up the sleep she'd lost.

It wasn't to be. As she rose from the table, Wyatt plucked her sweater off the peg and thrust it at her. "Hop over to the milkroom. Bridget's waiting for you."

"Hop?" Wasn't she due for a break? "Would it be all right if I just walked?"

Unperturbed, he threw on his own jacket. "As long as you get there."

"What do I do in the milkroom?"

"Enough to keep you busy till lunchtime."

"I can hardly wait." Concentrating all her skills on an attempt at ESP as she crossed the yard, she squeezed her eyes shut. "Dennis, wherever you are, save me."

Chapter Five

""Time to learn the cleaning process," a sunny-faced Bridget informed her as Gaby pinned her hat in place. "It's easy. We just flick these switches to run hot, soapy water, then clear, through the apparatus."

"Uh-hmm," Gaby said obligingly as the woman demonstrated.

"It's done after each milking. June has school, so she doesn't come in in the morning except on weekends."

"So I'm elected."

"When it's your turn."

"According to Wyatt's infamous schedule." Gaby was still smarting over his churlish attitude. Last night he'd kissed her as she'd never been kissed before. If she didn't know better, she'd think she'd been walking in her sleep, and it had all been a dream.

When the cleaning cycle was over, she and Bridget went to another room, where the woman demonstrated how to stamp expiration dates on moving bottles. Gaby's first dozen attempts had to be redone, but before long, she'd mastered it.

Next she used a heat gun to shrink plastic over the

bottle tops. If she held the gun too close, she ended with a shriveled mess. If she held it too far away, nothing happened. But at least this time, the King of the Mountain wasn't present to ridicule her fumbled attempts.

"How long did it take you to you master all this?" she asked Bridget, who did everything with so little effort.

"I grew up on a dairy farm. My father got tired of fighting the elements and gave it up for a city job. I'd already met my future husband by then. So when my folks left, we got married. I took this job to help make ends meet."

"Your husband is a farmer?"

"A schoolteacher who happens to love living in Woodbridge so much, he doesn't mind the commute."

"I haven't seen the plus side yet," Gaby said, not sure there was a plus side.

"I'll bet when your time is up, you won't want to go back to the city."

"That's a bet you're sure to lose."

When her assigned work was over, Gaby left by the side door, hoping for a moment to enjoy the day before she tackled another nerve-testing job.

To the left rose the Green Mountains. To the right were the shaded tiers of New York's Adirondacks. The sky was a sharp, cloudless blue, and the birdsong was a delight. Across the field waddled a fat little creature who paused now and then to nibble whatever looked tasty before going on.

"A porcupine?" she asked, spying Frank a few feet away, standing beside a piece of green-and-yellow farm machinery, scraping something off its blades with a metal tool.

"Ever seen one before?" he asked.

"In the zoo."

"Lots of wildlife in these parts."

"You Vermonters rave about your breathtaking scenery," she said, "then keep yourselves too busy to look at it."

"It might seem that way, Sunshine. But when you catch onto everything, you'll find time to pick daisies."

"I wish I could believe you. With your brother, it's two minutes for this, six for this. Put a move on. You're falling behind."

His laugh showed teeth that were as perfect as Wyatt's, except for a small chip between the front two. "Hurrying saves time for the fun."

"It sounds self-defeating." She crossed over to where he was working. "This is a tractor, I presume. When you have a minute, could you teach me to run it?" In her interview with Wyatt, he'd asked if she could drive one. For once, she'd like to surprise him and do something right the first time.

"It might take more than a minute," Frank warned.

"I learn quickly."

"Nothing like self-confidence." He dropped his tool on the bench. "Okay, Sunshine. Hop up."

"Now?"

"Why not?" He waited until she was seated, then began explaining the levers and pedals, before stepping up beside her. Then he went over it again, not behaving as if she were stupid when she asked questions. His voice might have been Wyatt's voice, she thought as she listened, except for a tad more good humor.

"Ready?" he asked.

Under his direction, she made two wide sweeps, with Frank only catching her hand twice to set her right. Then she came back and did two more with no help at all. Not until they'd returned to their starting place did she notice, to her chagrin, that Wyatt had arrived on the scene and was watching.

"Did you check out those rotted posts in the northwest section this morning?" he asked Frank, not commenting on Gaby's progress.

"Keep your shirt on, little brother. I wanted to show Gaby how this thing worked." Frank jumped down. "Now that you're a pro, Sunshine, why don't you practice on your own?"

"Not today," Wyatt said. "Marianne needs her help in the kitchen."

"I'll bet she does." Returning his glare with one better, she strode to the house, grumbling under her breath, to shell peas, snap beans, mop floors, or do one of the other thousand and one tasks that always needed doing.

Though she'd expected the day to drag, with so much to accomplish, it was exactly the opposite. Night was upon them before she knew it. By the time supper was over, she was so bone weary she wanted only to collapse in bed, no matter what direction the head or foot pointed.

Wyatt stepped out of the office as she passed. Fresh from her shower, she was clad in a bulky terry cloth robe, and her hair was bound in a towel turban. He, on the other hand, was distractingly handsome in a dark green shirt and a sports coat in a nubby weave. Why was it, she wondered wryly, that her breath never failed to catch in her throat when she came upon him unexpectedly?

Obviously he was going out. Since he hadn't been at the supper table, she assumed he was taking someone to dinner. Briefly, she pondered what it would be like to be in the spotlight of Wyatt's attentions.

To have him drive up to the house to collect her, with his hair neatly combed as it was now, and smelling of something delicious, splashed on just for her. To be the recipient of a mind-sweeping kiss, administered because he desired her lips on his, not because he wanted to prove a point.

That would be the day.

"No two-mile sprint tonight?" He feigned surprise.

"Too much wind," she shot back.

"Right." He grinned maddeningly and headed for the door. "It might blow you away."

"Cute," she muttered, trying not to waste any more

energy wondering about the lucky lady who would be graced by his presence.

The next morning was so clear and beautiful it was difficult to hold onto the notion that she was a prisoner. A sparrow chirped in the beech tree outside her window as she changed clothes after breakfast, and a red-tailed hawk sailed overhead as she returned to milkroom duty.

After breakfast, Wyatt was off as usual, looking for fence that needed patching. Gaby spied him stalking through the meadow, wearing a leather belt crammed with tools, a roll of wire over one arm, and an axe in his hand. That section, Frank had told her, was over eighty acres of woods and ravine. Should any animals stray into it, the family would have "one devil of a time rooting them out."

Gaby's own duty roster sent her to the lunchroom. Today she was being trusted to wait tables. Hector, her coworker, was a short, wiry man in his mid-twenties, with a droll sense of humor that kept her entertained as she learned what was expected of her.

Sophie, the woman in charge, was motherly, cheery, and undemanding. She'd worked for the Raffertys since she was a girl, she said, and had developed a great respect, if not affection, for Cole Rafferty, who asked a lot of his employees, but never more than he did of himself.

"His missus was about the prettiest girl I ever saw. Fair-haired as an angel and eyes like the sky. They loved each other fierce, and it was a sorry thing they weren't suited in more ways.''

''She didn't like the farm?''

''To put it mildly. She loved pretty clothes. Said she was born for them. Cole didn't see things her way. He thought she was being selfish when she wanted to shop for more dresses when she already had a closetful. And where would she wear them? Then she'd cry and complain that he never took her anywhere.''

''Sounds as if the marriage was doomed before it started,'' Gaby said, reinforcing in her mind her own warning when she arrived. Run—don't walk—away if you detect the slightest possibility of falling in love with the wrong person.

Who could be more wrong for her than Wyatt, who she suspected was an exact replica of his father?

When her shift was over, Sophie told her she'd done a good job. ''I look forward to working with you again, Gaby.''

Pshaw. A real, honest-to-goodness compliment? That was a first, Gaby mused on her way back to the house. Since things had gone well this far, maybe a day could pass without having to change her clothes. She was sick to death of denims. If she now had kitchen duty, she could put an apron over the outfit she was wearing.

''Wyatt asked me to send you out to the North Pasture.'' Marianne indicated a lunch basket. ''I've made turkey sandwiches, and there's a thermos and some caramel cake from last night.''

''No sit-down lunch today?''

''Beau's at school and Frank's working on the spreader. He'll grab something later. I have to make pies, so I already ate.''

''I'd better put on boots,'' Gaby said, thinking aloud. Though her tan pants were suitable for a trek across the field, and her bulky-knit cream sweater over her cotton shirt would be warm enough, her feet should have protection. The meadow grasses might be wet from a short rain the night before.

''Take the road as far as the fork.'' Marianne pointed through the window. ''You can cut across and save steps.''

''Thanks.''

''I made enough lunch for two.'' Had Marianne actually smiled at her? Things were looking up.

''Could I take a tablecloth?'' Wyatt wasn't a caveman. Surely he'd appreciate a touch of nicety. ''One of the plastic ones that wipe clean.''

''Take whatever you want.'' The woman was using a long-handled grasping tool for taking pie ingredients out of an overhead cabinet, and Gaby suppressed the offer to help. Marianne hated to be reminded of her limitations.

It was colder away from the shelter of the outbuildings, and Gaby was grateful for her sweater. She needn't have bothered combing her hair before she left, though. It blew every which way, and she gave up trying to keep it out of her eyes.

Wyatt, wearing a green-and-black plaid shirt unbuttoned over a fleece shirt, looked like a lumberjack. Certainly his build was powerful enough to qualify him for the job. He spotted her and leaned on his axe, waiting. "Don't you look fetching?" His skin glistened from exertion.

She might have returned the compliment if he'd been the amiable sort. "You're only saying that because I come bearing sandwiches." She glanced at a place where the land fell away, and a path covered with wood chips led down to an inviting pond. "Is the pond on Rafferty land? It would be a good place for a picnic."

He slapped a hand on the axe handle. "I wondered why you were so done up. You expect to have a picnic?"

"I'm not done up," she said, exasperated. "You have to stop and eat, unless you plan to swing that thing with one hand and eat your sandwich with the other. I even brought a tablecloth to make the meal festive."

"Festive," he echoed, as if the word were foreign. "Gaby, we're not here for a tea party. We have to fix that deadfall before dark."

"What's a deadfall?"

"Fallen trees lying crossways, making what looks like level ground." He demonstrated with his arms.

"An animal could stumble in and die. As a matter of fact, some inquisitive kid could do the same."

So what was she supposed to do about it?

"Put the basket down," he said, reading her question in her face. "I'll show you how to staple the wire in place. You'll follow me and reinforce what I wire together."

"I've used an office stapler many times."

"Not the same thing. You know how to hammer, don't you?"

"Doesn't everyone?"

Hiding her disappointment, she picked her way after him, down a slope thick with brambles and wild strawberries. "Marianne didn't tell me . . . Ouch. Wait." She stopped to pull her pants leg where it had snagged on a thorn. An inch of fabric was ripped in a place where it couldn't be mended. To make matters worse, her knee was scratched.

"Why didn't you wear something on your legs?" Wyatt barked.

"I'm wearing pants."

"The kind you'd wear to a garden party."

"I wouldn't wear pants to a garden party. After living in them here, I don't know if I'll ever wear them again."

He stopped at a place where the cross rails gave way to barbed wire, some of it dark and rusty. She couldn't even see through the tangle.

"That's an odd fence," she said. "Wire, wood,

whatever. It's hard to tell what starts where. How can you mend it in a way that'll look right?''

He snorted. ''We're not after beauty here, Gaby. We use whatever serves.''

''I would think—''

''Forget what you think.'' He dipped his head in mock appreciation. ''Granted you look very pretty. ''But I'd trade Miss Beauty Queen in an instant for a competent helper.''

She could feel her face coloring. ''I'm competent.''

''This is a two-man job. It's why I sent for you.''

''Two *man*?''

''Man—woman. It isn't a matter of strength. In fact, Marianne is better at this than Frank or me. Be careful. Some of that wire's sharp and not easily seen.''

''Tell me about it,'' she said, checking the stinging scratch on her leg again.

He shook his head. ''That sweater looks thin. What's it made out of—silk?''

''I didn't realize there was a dress code. Maybe I should buy long johns.''

''You'll be wearing them come winter.'' He considered her through narrowed eyes. ''If you're still here.''

''When Marianne sent me with the lunch basket, I didn't expect to be working.''

''You thought you'd provide decoration?''

Why did he take pleasure in putting her down? ''Of course not.''

''You thought I needed company?''

"No," she snapped. "I'd be the last person you'd call for company. You'll notice at least, I'm wearing boots."

"Boots," he hooted. "With velvet tops."

"It's not velvet. They're rain boots."

"Made for tripping a few feet from your car to your apartment."

"Never mind the way I'm dressed," she said, flaring up. "Everything I'm wearing is washable. I can do what's expected of me the way I am."

"If you say so." He thrust the hammer at her, along with a box of heavy staples. "Hit as directly as you can, and be careful of your fingers."

"Right."

"Watch where you step," he said, setting off.

"Wait," she called to his back, struggling to free herself from a spot where her foot had sunk deeply into the mud. One step was all she could manage. "This is like quicksand. I—I can't get my foot out."

"Now what?" he asked the graying clouds overhead. Dropping his axe, he returned to where she was standing. Leaning her forward so she was lying across his shoulder, he yanked her foot free, leaving the boot behind.

"I could have done that much."

He scratched his head. "Don't move until I—"

Before he'd finished his admonition, she lost her balance, stepped back into the clay with her bootless foot, and sat down hard. "Yikes, it's—it's cold!" she shrieked.

Growling, he caught her up again, this time working one arm around her shoulders and the other under her knees. After reaching down to retrieve the shoe she'd left behind, he carried her to higher ground. "You'll have to hightail it back to the house before you get pneumonia."

"There's mud inside my boot. How am I supposed to walk?"

"You expect me to carry you piggyback?"

"I don't know what I expect," she said miserably.

"Well, I can't. I won't." He looked down at her for a long moment, his eyes gleaming in the stabbing sun rays. Shifting her so she was facing him, he allowed her to slide down enough to take her own weight.

"Thank you," she tried, but her teeth were chattering so hard, no sound came out. Her breath came in spasms.

"You're like ice." This time he didn't step away or bark orders. He only drew her close, close, closer. "What am I going to do with you?"

"I—I don't know."

"I think you do." His face was still composed, but his voice was raw.

"Yes," she admitted, her blood surging like a mountain cataract as his arms tightened around her.

His wonderful mouth, familiar now, lowered to capture hers. Though seconds ago she'd believed she was too frozen to move, she slid her arms around his neck easily in automatic response, and heat whipped through her. If this was the measure of a kiss, she'd never been kissed before.

"I can't leave now, but you have to get inside," he said almost angrily. He administered another brief, hard kiss before dropping his arms to his sides. "Go back to the house the best you can. Take a hot shower and put something on that scratch, so it doesn't get infected."

"I'm not cold." She waited, hoping he would kiss her again. Then she'd be able to walk back to the house without her feet touching the ground.

"What's holding you? Wasn't that appreciation enough for you?" His gaze hardened into a glare.

"I don't expect appreciation." She blinked.

"I suppose it's hard to be young and beautiful and have nobody notice. Unfortunately, out here, Beau's too young, Frank's married, and there's only me to hand out the compliments. I'm not sure I want to take on the job."

"Who asked you?" Her face must have been flaming. "I prefer to be appreciated for what I accomplish."

"So let's accomplish something. Change into sensible clothes and get back here before the sun goes down."

The walk across the field with humiliation washing over her and freezing mud squishing between her toes seemed interminable. Before she stepped on the porch, she scraped all the dirt she could off the sides of her boots and the soles. The lining would have to wait until she got to the bathroom.

Not trusting herself to look at Marianne, she stormed inside, knowing she wouldn't be able to contain bitter words if she saw the smug smile curving on the woman's wide mouth.

"Don't track anything in," Marianne sang. "You'll need a couple of wash loads to take care of just your own laundry, the way things are going. What happened?"

"Isn't it obvious?"

"You have to watch ground in that section. It's like a swamp."

Silently counting to ten, Gaby limped to her room, where she gathered up a fresh set of clothes and went in to take a shower. Within a half an hour, she was bundled up and back in the field. Wyatt made no comment about what had happened and neither did she, except to promise herself it wouldn't happen again.

Pleased with herself for setting Gaby up for ridicule, Marianne kept up a chatter at the supper table as they ate fried chicken, browned new potatoes, and fresh green beans. She talked about her new quilt, a Dresden plate design that was nearly finished, and about an old friend who'd stopped by for a visit that morning.

"The years haven't been kind. I hardly recognized

her.'' She laughed dryly. ''Or maybe she's saying the same thing about me.''

''You still look like a schoolgirl, honey,'' Frank assured her. ''Doesn't she, Beau?''

''She looks okay.'' The boy reached for the green beans.

''I can't get over Vermont weather,'' Gaby tried, breaking into the conversation to show the Raffertys that their worst couldn't dampen her spirits.

''Is that good or bad?'' Wyatt asked.

''It's invigorating.'' She curled her toes inside her shoes, rethinking what he'd said to her in the field about her ''need to be appreciated,'' and how he wasn't sure he wanted to take on the job.

Well, she wasn't offering it to him, and she ached for the next opportunity to tell him so.

''The weather's warm all the time where you come from, isn't it, Gaby?'' Beau asked. ''Swimming every day, if you want. Going out on a boat.''

''If I can find the time.''

''I hear you drove the tractor today. Nice going.''

''Your father's a good teacher.'' She smiled at Frank. At least she had one friend. Two, counting Beau. ''My first car had a stick shift. That experience helped.''

Probably afraid she'd get too big for her blue jeans if the compliments continued, Wyatt began talking about parts they needed for a planter, and how someone was going to have to go see about renting a fertilizer. From what Gaby gathered, though they had their own equipment, it was cheaper to use someone else's. Marianne agreed to make arrangements in the morning.

Wasn't it enough to work twelve hours a day without taking work to the table with them? Farmers indulged in the same bonhomie as lawyers and other professionals, leaving no room for anyone else.

"I'd like to learn about Vermont birdlife. Is there a library in Woodbridge?" she asked, determined to stay in the conversation.

"We have a bookmobile," Marianne said. "It stops in town every other Friday morning. You can order any book you want."

"And get gray-haired waiting for it to arrive," Beau hooted.

"How about a movie theater?" Gaby asked.

"It's only open on Saturday," the boy said out of the corner of his mouth. "And it's not half filled then. People in these parts aren't much for wanting a good time. Anything showing there you probably saw years ago. Woodbridge folks still refer to them as 'moving picture shows.' "

"Or talkies?" Gaby said, and they laughed together.

Looking insulted, Marianne pressed her lips together. "We have plenty of recreation. Fairs, barbecue suppers, visiting . . ."

"Mostly visiting," Beau broke in. "Call sitting

around, talking about the weather having a good time?"

Frank grinned and turned to Gaby. "I imagine you feel at loose ends away from the city. Did you meet June? Maybe you can hang around with her while you're here."

"Maybe," she agreed amicably, though she was sure the teenaged milkroom worker had enough chums without taking on an 'older woman.'

"We won't let Wyatt keep you chained to the cowshed," Frank went on. "Sometimes he forgets young people need a day of fun. Burlington's only a little over an hour away."

"I understand there're only about forty thousand people there," she said.

"Only?" Beau growled.

"I meant that it isn't a huge metropolis," Gaby added quickly, realizing that in her attempt to join in the conversation, she'd stirred up Beau's discontent. It was easy to see that he wasn't enthusiastic about his life on the dairy farm either.

"Only forty thousand in the city proper," Frank said. "But since it's a college town, you can add fifteen thousand students, as well as another hundred thousand in surrounding communities."

"It might be fun to visit." To go shopping and to a genuine restaurant where she'd be waited on, and not have to peel potatoes, set the table, and do the dishes.

"I wouldn't be adverse to a day in the city myself," Marianne said.

"You'll have one," Frank assured her. "As soon as Gaby knows the routine enough to take over without supervision."

Marianne didn't look as if she thought it was possible. "We'll see."

"I notice you have a VCR." Gaby turned her attention back to Beau. "You can always rent the latest films and invite friends over to watch, can't you?"

"By the time he does his chores and his schoolwork," Marianne said, "he doesn't have time for that kind of thing."

"That's for sure. No time for anything but work, work, work," Beau growled. "May I be excused?"

"You haven't had dessert yet," his mother protested.

"May I be excused?" Without waiting for an answer, he was gone.

Wyatt didn't say anything but looked at Gaby as if she were responsible for the boy's flare-up.

Why not? I'm responsible for everything else that goes wrong around here.

Beau's door was open as she passed later. He'd been drawing but put a book over his paper as she approached.

"Do you know if there's an extra alarm clock I could use?" she asked.

"Mom's got an old one in the kitchen cabinet, top shelf. Over the bread box. But it's not electric."

"That's okay."

"You don't mind the tick-tocking all night?"

"Not at all." She walked over to where he was sitting and slid the book aside. On a large piece of graph paper he'd sketched what looked like a depiction of Notre Dame cathedral. "You did this?"

He shrugged. "I was only messing around. It's fun to work things out to scale."

"But not easy."

"It is for me." He reached in the bottom drawer of his desk and brought out other sketches.

"You're very good," she said, impressed.

"I work on the school paper and design most of the posters. You know, letting the other kids know what's happening? In fact, I designed the yearbook cover." He brought out an annual that showed a school with a clock tower, trees, and a busy campus.

"This is fantastic," she said truthfully. She'd had friends in second-year art classes who couldn't have done nearly as well. "I hope you do something with your talent."

"What can I do around here?"

"No law says you have to stay in Woodbridge when you've graduated. Doesn't Burlington have an art school?"

"I wouldn't mind going to Parson's School of Design in New York.'' He grimaced. ''But who can afford that?''

So he *had* considered a career in art. ''Work hard and get a scholarship. I have a friend who can look into it for you, and collect brochures, and such. You should talk to your counselor.''

''Think so?'' The boy looked pleased.

''Definitely.''

His face changed as he looked past her, and she knew that not only was someone standing at the door, but who the someone was. Wyatt.

''Good night, Beau.'' She squeezed his shoulder. ''Keep up the good work.''

Wyatt didn't speak until he'd trailed her to the end of the hall. When he did, his voice was a threatening rumble. ''I'd appreciate it if you didn't interfere in family affairs. You'll only cause trouble.''

''Why would it cause trouble to encourage your nephew to follow his dreams?''

Wyatt's eyes sent out green sparks. ''We're farmers in this house. Not dreamers.''

''You have something against dreams?''

''Not dreams that have a solid foundation.''

''On Rafferty Farms there are rules for dreams, too?''

The pause that followed lasted a good ten seconds. ''I'm telling you to keep out of it. Understood?''

He wheeled away, but this time, she followed *him*. ''You remind me of Ben Cartwright.''

''Who?''

"On the old TV show *Bonanza*. Cartwright had three sons—grown men—who did everything he said without arguing. As if they didn't have minds of their own. It was always, 'Yes, Pa,' and 'No, Pa.' Never mind what they thought or what they wanted to do with their lives.''

The bones stood out sharply under his skin. His jaw clenched, and suddenly she wished she hadn't said anything. ''Somebody has to take charge of a business like this or it goes under. You wouldn't understand.''

''No, I'm afraid I wouldn't,'' she agreed, watching him stalk away.

Later, as she lay in bed, she held her book in a reading position, determined to engross herself in the plot. But no matter how hard she tried, she found herself thinking of Wyatt, and how his anger at her had smoldered.

The next thing she knew, she'd fallen asleep. She might have slept that way all night except for the noise. There was no rain, but a high wind was whistling through the eaves and crashing through the yard, rearranging everything that wasn't nailed down.

She crept out of bed and crossed to the window, just in time to see a cardboard box fly past and flatten against the barn. A small funnel like a miniature tornado fascinated her, and she half expected it to grow until it was large enough to pick up the house.

When it didn't, she returned to bed and pulled the second quilt up to her chin. The Rafferty house had seen its share of wind in the generations since it was built, she assured herself. It would stand for a few more.

Again she dreamt she was waiting for a bus. Again it didn't stop for her. Again she chased after it, yelling for the driver to come back. This time Wyatt was inside, laughing at her.

Chapter Six

Thanks to her borrowed clock, Gaby was out of bed before Wyatt's fist hit the door.

"I'm up," she called, pulling on the jeans and sweatshirt she'd arranged across the back of a chair the night before. After winding a scarf around her hair, she was in the kitchen, reaching for her cup. She still didn't like coffee, but at least it was hot.

Frank was her partner that day. Wyatt would be working on the coupler for most of the morning, and Beau was in the milkroom, whistling something unrecognizable. It pleased Gaby to think that maybe she'd lightened the boy's heart by offering encouragement. Until she'd lived under the same roof with Wyatt, she hadn't realized how vital encouragement could be.

Frank worked one aisle while she worked the other, and though they carried on a conversation, she almost kept up with him.

"Nice going, Sunshine," he said when they were finished. "You're a born dairy farmer."

"I have better luck when your brother isn't watching."

"Don't let Wyatt get you down."

87

"Don't worry about me. I'm unsinkable," she said, trying to believe it.

"It's nothing personal. He distrusts summer people and you're in the same category." Frank's eyes were disturbingly like his brother's when they were serious. "Here today, gone tomorrow. Or in your case, when your contract is fulfilled. He doesn't want to get too close."

"If I can make the best of the situation, why can't he?" She wanted to ask why Wyatt hated her, but decided it would sound histrionic.

"It was difficult for him when my mother left. He was only ten." Frank squirted soap on his hands and handed the plastic dispenser to Gaby. "She didn't have the heart to tell him good-bye, so she left a note on his pillow, saying she loved him with all her heart, but she'd go mad if she stayed any longer."

Gaby thought of the photograph she'd seen of Priscilla and Cole Rafferty's wedding. Happy expectancy shone in the eyes of the young couple who didn't realize yet how tragic a mismatch it would be.

"When Wyatt woke up, he took off after her," Frank went on. "The whole town turned out to search for him, but it was a good thirty-six hours before they located him in a barn about ten miles away, almost frozen. It was the last time I ever saw him cry."

Tears formed in Gaby's eyes as she thought of the sad little boy who'd become a difficult man. She blinked them away. ''It must have been hard on you, too.''

Frank thrust out his lower lip, an expression that also reminded her of Wyatt. ''I was older. Six years makes a whale of a difference in kids. I'd known for a long time Mom was unhappy. Dairy farming is hard on women.''

''Marianne doesn't mind.''

''She grew up to the life, like Wyatt and I did.''

''But unlike your brother, you admit there's another world out there. Will you leave some day?''

''Not a chance. I feel uprooted when I'm away.''

''We'd better get to breakfast before Marianne calls again.'' She dried her hands and tossed the paper towel into the trash can. ''She's a great cook, but I'd still prefer a steaming bowl of soup for breakfast. And why not? It's hot and nourishing.''

''A preference for chicken noodle soup is constitutional, as far as I know.''

''Sometimes I wonder,'' she said grimly.

He waited for her to pass, then shut the door and slid the lockpin into place. ''I'm driving to Woodbridge after lunch to pick up some machine parts. If you want to ride along and stock up on some of that soup, you're welcome.''

Gaby felt light-headed, as if she'd just won a trip to Paris. ''Super. I only saw the town once when I arrived, and I didn't actually see it then.''

"You'll like it. We have some good people in Woodbridge."

The house was chilly, in spite of the heat generated by breakfast preparations. Gaby remarked on it as she took her place at the table.

"A window broke during the night," Marianne said tightly. She jerked her head toward the pass-through, where the curtains had been taken down.

Gaby wasn't surprised. "The wind?"

"It picked up the rake you left leaning against the house and hurled it through the glass. Wyatt's been most of the morning fixing it. He had trouble getting a pane the right size."

Ouch. Gaby cringed at finding herself in trouble again. "Are you sure I did it?"

"No one else raked yesterday."

"I'm sorry." She was beginning to think she should wear a sign with a printed apology.

Frank reached for a biscuit and spread apricot jam on it. "Gaby's not used to our windstorms."

"She's from Florida," Marianne countered. "They have so many hurricanes, they give them names to tell them apart."

"Remember to put your tools away," Wyatt said, as if she hadn't received the message loud and clear already. "They can cause a lot of damage."

"I see on the duty roster, you'll be mixing chocolate milk today," Beau remarked, rescuing her from a lengthier lecture. "That's one job I like."

"Because you drink more than you bottle," his mother said.

Frank raised an eyebrow. "More likely because he has a yen for our little June Weems."

Beau grinned and didn't offer a denial.

"Watch those older women, son," Frank teased. "They can be a handful."

"June's only a year older than me."

"A year and a half," Marianne corrected. "Besides, girls mature quicker."

Beau's face reddened. "It doesn't matter. She's already got a boyfriend."

"Since when did that stop you from trying?"

Wyatt was unusually quiet. His eyes had barely brushed Gaby's as he warned her about the rake. She couldn't help wondering if he was stewing over what she'd said to him about trying to run his nephew's life. Hadn't anyone ever criticized him before? Then it was about time.

When Beau had left for school, and Marianne went to the restaurant, Gaby set off for the milkroom again. Though she was a chocolate lover, before she and Bridget had finished measuring cocoa and sugar, mixing and bottling, the smell had given her a headache.

Feeling the need for a breath of fresh air, she went outside and wandered across the yard, where the Rafferty dog, Legs, a comical mix with a setter's body but disproportionately long legs, was snoozing in a patch of sun. When she stooped to scratch his head, a station wagon swerved around the half circle of driveway, screeched to a stop, and a petite blond got out.

She wore frontier pants, and her gleaming hair bounced against her shoulders as she walked. Wyatt trotted out to meet her, and they talked at length.

''That's Ruth Ann Dougherty,'' Bridget said, joining Gaby outside. ''Cute as a bug, isn't she? Her parents own the Country Store. A couple of years ago, she left for college. Her folks wanted her to be a vet. But she got homesick and came back. If you want to know the truth, I think it was Wyatt she missed, not the old homestead.''

''She doesn't look more than sixteen,'' Gaby said, experiencing a curious sense of resentment.

''She's twenty, going on forty. She trailed after Wyatt like Mary's little lamb when she was in pinafores. Now, if you'll notice, he isn't running away.''

No, he wasn't. The girl was even making him laugh. Not an easy task. She slapped at him playfully, and he pointed a finger at her.

''She'll catch him eventually.''

''What makes you say that?''

''He's a man. He's past thirty and I know he loves kids. He'll want some of his own soon.''

''To help with the farm, no doubt,'' Gaby said, thinking that cute-as-a-bug Ruth Ann was welcome to him. Would he let them lie around for the first year of their lives before he put them on the work roster?

Later, he wasn't at lunch. Nobody offered an explanation, and she wasn't about to ask. Assuming that he'd gone off with Ruth Ann since her station wagon disappeared at the same time he did, she was surprised to see him in the driver's seat of the truck, instead of his brother.

"Frank told me he had to drive to Woodbridge and asked if I wanted to go along," she explained.

"He told me, too. But he remembered something else he had to do."

"What about the parts he needed to pick up?"

"I've got the list." He patted his pocket. "Sure you want to go? Not much there to appeal to a woman like you."

"A woman like me?"

"A woman who's seen everything—done everything." He reached across to open the door for her.

"I'm not that jaded. You must be thinking of somebody else."

A corner of his mouth twitched. "I don't think so."

"I want to learn all there is about the place where I'll be living for the next year."

"What will you do when you're free here?" he asked when she'd climbed in beside him, and they were on their way.

"That depends. Will I get time off for good behavior?"

"Not a chance."

"You're a hard-hearted jailer."

A muscle moved in his cheek, making her wonder

if it had been wise to joke with him. "You think of yourself as being in jail?"

"Not really," she admitted, watching the meadow-land and wide-spreading trees fly past the window. "Farm life isn't as terrible as I expected it to be, and this part of the country is beautiful."

"You say that because you haven't experienced a Vermont winter."

"I know what to expect. I've read books, and I've seen movies set in Vermont."

"And we know how accurately life is depicted on the screen." He slowed to allow a squirrel to skitter across. "You didn't answer about your plans when you return to civilization."

"I guess I'll continue where I left off. I know I can contribute to my uncle's company, or any company I join."

He glanced at her, then back at the road, "That's it? With your talk about dreams, I expected yours to be more elaborate."

"Eventually I'll run my own business. That's not as farfetched as it sounds, seeing as I don't have a lot of capital."

"How will you swing it?"

"There's a trend these days for companies to farm work out."

"Farm out—how?" he asked, as if it mattered.

"They've learned that they can cut down on over-head and labor costs by helping qualified workers start on their own, then doing business with them. Many companies conduct free seminars and offer free or low-cost leasing of equipment.''

''So you want to be your own boss. Why doesn't that surprise me?''

''It shouldn't,'' she tossed back at him, ''any more than I'd be surprised that you need to be at the head of your own operation.''

''Like Ben Cartwright.'' His unexpected grin drew one from her. Maybe he wasn't holding a grudge.

In a much shorter time than she'd anticipated—too short, considering how well they were getting along—they passed the marker that welcomed them to Woodbridge. Wyatt parked in front of the city hall with its obligatory clock tower. Together they crossed the square, an area divided by a walkway that began at a sundial and divided to skirt freshly dug flower beds. Straight ahead was a Victorian hotel, like something out of a gothic novel, with a peaked roof, balconies, and curlicued decorations on the windows.

It was a charming little town with an honest-to-goodness bandstand and shops that had either been built at the turn of the century, or were fashioned to look as if they had. Gaby could only imagine how charming a scene it would make decorated with a layer of snow.

''Stocks?'' she questioned, stopping to read an historical marker next to a platform that held weathered boards cut out to fit over the neck and wrists of long-ago miscreants. "They actually used this contraption?"

"You'd better believe it."

"Does it give you any ideas for employee management?"

"One or two." Wyatt's grin was one-sided.

"I wish I'd brought my camera."

"There'll be other times." He hooked his thumbs over the back pockets of his jeans. "You have an hour to browse before we have to start back."

"That should be more than enough time," she said, looking around to get her bearings.

Walking the two-block-long main street wouldn't have taken more than a few minutes, she thought as Wyatt went in one direction, and she went in the other. But on an impulse, she stopped in the shops to introduce herself, though it was apparent from the first that everybody already knew her identity.

Her favorite store, Deke's Odds and Ends, carried everything from greeting cards to hubcaps, to barrels of penny candy, and used furniture. Browsing kept her so intrigued, she almost forgot her time limit. She'd just finished buying a map of the countryside sketched on canvas when Wyatt leaned on his horn, alerting her that her hour was up.

"With your hectic schedule, I don't suppose you'd ever have time for travel," she said when they were heading home. "Doesn't it bother you that you'll never see the world?"

"No reason why I shouldn't see it someday. That's the advantage of a partnership. Marianne and Frank can handle things with the help of hired hands when I feel the need for a vacation. Of course, when Pete was here, it was easier."

It was the first time he'd mentioned him, and it caught her off guard. "Don't you have a dream, Wyatt?"

He nodded. "It's right here. The family working together. Helping people. Helping ourselves to the good life."

She might have known his dream would revolve around the farm. She dug in her handbag and brought out the square of canvas. "A map of the area for tourists," she explained. "I like to know where I am."

"And where you're going."

"You've got that right." She pointed. "That's Hill Road? Where's the hill?" The road sign was too weather-beaten to read.

He smiled crookedly. "Hill was the family name. The house was struck by lightning and burned about ten years ago, but the name stuck."

"What happened to the Hills?"

"They scattered when the daughters got married. The old man didn't have the heart to rebuild when his wife died, so he stayed in the hotel."

"There's supposed to be a covered bridge." She tapped a finger on the map.

Wyatt slowed and turned off the main road onto one

that was more of a cow path. The truck rose and fell as it bounced over the ruts.

"Where are we going?"

"You wanted to see the bridge."

"Since when are you so obliging?" she asked, surprised.

"I'm always obliging when the circumstances call for it."

"Meaning that I've stopped bellyaching?"

"Exactly." He pulled to a stop and came around to open the door for her before she could manage it herself.

The excitement of discovery grew as they strolled toward the quaint structure of wooden arches and supports, their fingers brushing lightly with their movement. But anticipation quickly evaporated.

"It's so dilapidated," she groaned, disappointed. "How did it stand up to that last windstorm?"

"Years of hard weather caused what you see."

She stepped gingerly onto the first plank but jumped back when it creaked with her weight. "Where's the water?"

"Rerouted for irrigation years ago," he said, steadying her.

Would he suppose that bumping into him was her way of flirting? Maybe not. He seemed less uptight today. "That's terrible. The structure should have been preserved."

"People had good intentions. But years passed and there was always too much else to do."

By silent consent, they continued up a gentle rise to where they could gaze out over a checkerboard of neat farms, a meandering stream, and a pine woods beyond. To their left was a handsome sycamore tree, whose leaves were brilliant with spring greening. Ahead stood what was left of Hill House. At this distance it looked intact.

Gaby hugged herself. "It's colder here than it is over there."

"The winds change from moment to moment."

She shook her head. "It's more. As if something tragic happened in this spot."

"Your imagination is working overtime. The land doesn't change according to the vicissitudes of human fate."

"I'm not so sure. I read once about a spot where a girl died tragically. The grass never grew again."

"That sort of story is good around a campfire." He bent down and pulled up a spindly plant. A miniature potato clung to its roots. "Mr. Hill was proud of his potatoes. Claimed he grew the best in the state."

"Did he?"

"Should we cook this one and find out?" he offered.

"I don't think Marianne would appreciate it," she said ruefully. Leaving him on the ridge, she wandered alone over to the sycamore and spread her arms wide, as if to embrace the moment. "This would make a perfect spot for a picnic."

He chuckled softly. "What's with you and picnics?"

"I've always loved them. There's an intimacy in sharing a basket of good things with a friend that can't be matched, even by an atmosphere of candle glow and soft music."

"I'll take a steak any time." He positioned his fingers two inches apart to indicate the thickness he'd prefer.

"Make mine spaghetti and meatballs."

"Good choice. As long as I'm sitting at a table in a comfortable chair."

"You don't mean that. Where's the Rafferty spirit of adventure?" She smoothed a hand along the roughness of the tree's bark and peered closer. "Someone carved initials."

"Nothing so romantic." He strolled over to stand beside her. "It's a scar, left by an injury to the wood when it was small."

"I like my explanation better." She met his gaze squarely, thinking how much more she'd like to learn about this man, if he'd allow it. "Were you ever in love, Wyatt? I mean, when you were a child. Was there a little girl with springy curls and ruffly dresses who captured your heart?"

"Not that I can remember."

"All you could think about was the farm, even then?"

He chewed on his lower lip. "For a while I wanted to be a ballplayer."

That was a start. "Were you any good?"

He shrugged. "I thought I was."

"So what happened?"

He dropped the potato, brushed off his hands, and looked toward the road. "Where are we going with this line of questioning?"

Undaunted by his tone, she forged ahead. "I told you. I like to know the town where I'll be spending the next year of my life. And I like to know the people."

"Why are you trying so hard?"

"To be friends, you mean? I see no reason for us to live in the same house, sit at the same table, and glare at each other. I'm harmless."

"Said Lorelei to the boatmen she lured to their doom." He looked serious.

"Do I look capable of doing that?"

"Definitely." He studied her with such intensity, she felt as if she were under a microscope. "I know you. You were the little girl who brought apples to the teacher."

She cocked her head to one side, wondering how he'd guessed so much about her. Was it possible that she was in his thoughts as often as he was in hers? "With me it was roses. My mother had a prize garden."

"You had to be sure the teacher liked you."

"What makes you say that?"

"Because you're still that little girl. Here you stand, looking at me with eyes as blue as a summer sky, begging for acceptance."

"I don't need your acceptance."

"Then it's something else you want."

One step, and another, brought him dangerously close. She took the same amount of steps back. If he was talking about the appreciation he'd mentioned before, along with another kiss, it would be impossible to offer a sincere denial. Lately she hadn't been able to catch sight of him without remembering how his mouth had felt on hers.

"Another thing about Vermont," she said haltingly. "It grows gigantic egos."

"It isn't my ego talking." He closed the gap again.

"We'd better go." This time when she reached back with her toe, she found she had no more escape room. She was nearly wedged against the tree. "We'll be late for milking."

"I don't think so." His eyes seared her mouth.

"Those are daffodils, aren't they?" Disquieted, she swept a glance past his shoulder toward blooms that appeared to be a solid blanket of yellow. "Maybe we could gather them for the table."

"Another time." He braced one hand against the tree over her head and dipped down to capture her lips easily in a numbing kiss. Closing her eyes, she swayed against him, wanting to hold onto the sensation that slithered through her.

"Someone might pass by," she whispered, needing to say something.

It wasn't a proper protest, she realized dizzily. She should have asked him to stop because . . . because . . . she couldn't remember why she should. Her eyelids felt so heavy she couldn't keep them open as he began a fresh assault on her mouth.

"We aren't so different after all," she murmured, struggling to get her breath.

"You're wrong, Gaby." His voice broke with the pronouncing of her name.

"Wrong about what?"

"About our not being different."

He wouldn't burst the bubble now. He couldn't. "If you believe that, why did you kiss me?"

"We've been moving toward this since you got off the bus."

"You felt it, too?" She'd known he had, even then. The sight of him had hit like a fist in her middle, and she'd tried to attribute it to her arrival in a strange place.

"Yes, I did." A warning colored his voice. The other Wyatt—the one who seemed to enjoy hurting her—had returned again. "But it isn't going to happen. Not now. Not ever. Save your sighs for someone who wants them."

With effort, her determination swam to the surface. "I didn't expect anything to happen."

Only a trace of his former softness remained in his eyes as he lifted her chin gently with his index finger. "As you said, we have to get back for the milking. That should hold you for a while."

She flattened her hands against his chest and pushed. "Stop pretending you kissed me only for my sake. We both know it isn't true." She couldn't have been so wrong about the shared emotion.

"Denial wouldn't change the facts."

"And don't kiss me again," she cried, choking back tears. "Or I'll make your sorry you did."

"I won't. If you don't look at me the way you looked a moment ago."

"How did I look?"

"As if you came here today, hoping it would happen."

"So you say," she shot back, moving double-time toward the car. "We'll never know, will we?"

"You're right," he admitted as he turned the key in the ignition. His tone was as stiff as it had been the morning he warned her to stay out of family business. "Forget it happened."

"It's already forgotten," she lied, and they drove back to the farm in silence.

Chapter Seven

As the days turned to weeks, milking was still Gaby's least favorite chore. The bovine inhabitants of Rafferty Farms, like their human counterparts, knew they had the upper hand and she practically had to beg for cooperation. Still, she'd become passably proficient.

She was taking regular shifts at the lunchroom, too, not only waiting on tables, but dicing vegetables, making sandwiches, and delivering milk to the outlets. Most of the customers were friendly and she was getting to know them by name.

Marianne, whose cast had been exchanged for a smaller one, was still curt but had cut down on her snipping. Even Wyatt hadn't leapt down Gaby's throat lately, though his disapproval seethed beneath the surface.

Now and then, when they were paired together on a chore, he made no move to kiss, or even touch her, but ghosts of their disagreement floated back and forth between them.

Though the calendar claimed it was June, the frost that carpeted the ground in the morning made it hard to believe. Then the county fair Beau had talked about since her arrival was upon them.

"You're going, aren't you, Gaby?" he asked when they sat down to breakfast on the big morning.

"She wouldn't be interested in our little backcountry doings." Marianne started the French toast around the table and followed it with a jug of maple syrup.

"They have Disney World in Florida," Wyatt reminded his nephew. "Woodbridge can't compete."

Beau looked crushed. "I forgot."

"I'm looking forward to the fair." Gaby ladled tomato soup into her bowl. At last this idiosyncrasy was accepted and not commented upon. "The theme attractions are fun. But my favorite ride has always been the carousel. And I adore cotton candy."

"All right," Beau yelped with enthusiasm. "I'm helping out in the livestock tent, so I have to get there early. When you join the team, you get free rides and half price on food."

"They'll be sorry they made that deal with you," Marianne teased. "You'll eat your weight in hot dogs."

"You could make a mint in the kissing booth, Gaby," Beau blurted without thinking, then blushed.

"Do they have one?" she asked, avoiding eye contact with Wyatt.

"I don't know," Frank said jovially, using knife and fork to cut his French toast into neat squares. "But it wouldn't be a bad idea."

Marianne's lips tightened, but she made no comment.

"Mom's donated some super-pies and one of her quilts is up for a prize. Bet she wins big this year."

"Remember, everybody." Wyatt donned his Simon Legree frown. "Tomorrow we'll have to—"

"Work twice as hard to make up lost time," Beau finished for him. "Who cares? It'll be worth it."

Since Bridget and her husband had already taken Beau to the fairgrounds by the time morning chores were completed, Frank drove the camper, allowing Marianne more legroom. Wyatt, Gaby, and Hector took the truck. Two vehicles were needed because some-one—a short straw appointed Frank—had to ride back in a few hours and check on the husband-and-wife team they had hired for the evening milking. Other-wise, the day was free.

Frank gave a low whistle as Gaby stepped off the porch. "All spiffed up, eh, Sunshine?"

She struck a pose. "It feels good to wear a dress again." The one she'd chosen for today was firecracker red and sleeveless, with a tie in back, and a skirt that barely brushed her knees.

"You look like a million dollars, doesn't she, Wyatt?" Frank persisted.

"She looks very nice," Wyatt said without en-thusiasm.

Hector, whose new girlfriend was meeting him at the ticket booth, kept the conversation alive as they rode, allowing Gaby to gaze at the winding rock wall that bordered the road on their way, without contributing.

A high school band was playing as they drove through the gates. A cheer went up as multicolored balloons were released and someone set off fireworks, though the main display wouldn't take place until that evening. Marianne and Frank headed for the building that housed the exhibits. Hector went to meet his lady-love. That left Wyatt and Gaby alone.

He looked spiffy himself, she couldn't help musing, in a deep blue shirt, open at the collar, loose-fitting slacks, and a lightweight sports coat in deference to the rising temperature.

"No need for you to be stuck with me," she told him, as if she couldn't care less. "If you have something better to do, I can amuse myself."

"Trying to get rid of me?"

"No, but . . ."

"Why don't we start here and work our way around the perimeter?"

"You plan to take in everything?" She hadn't thought of him as an enthusiastic participant.

"Any objections?"

"None." Maybe he was volunteering to see the fair with her out of a sense of duty. Maybe not. Either way, she wasn't about to turn him down.

He took her arm with an exaggerated display of chivalry. "Then let's go."

After they'd tried their luck at the rifle range, without winning anything, and dart-throwing, again walking away without a prize, a man guessed their combined weights, right on the money, and a woman in a spangled veil told their fortunes.

"What did she say?" Gaby asked as they stopped for cotton candy.

"I'll climb many mountains and meet the love of my life under unusual circumstances." His rakish smile had all the effects of a sweet, slow kiss from anyone else.

"Sounds romantic," she stammered.

"How about you?"

"A big change is right around the corner."

"So what do you think?" He leaned close with an expression of shared confidentiality that warmed her to the soles of her feet. "Is she a genuine seer?"

"The change she mentioned has already pounced on me." Admittedly Gaby wasn't the same person who'd kissed Dennis good-bye at the bus station. If that was the change she meant, Madame Theda was a tad late. "Are you planning to climb any mountains in the near future?"

"I've already encountered a few." His gaze rested on her lips briefly. "Hungry?"

"A little."

"Better be ravenous, unless you want to insult the cooks."

Inside a huge tent, filled with delicious smells, booths had been set up everywhere. Smiling women with trays pressed minute cups of spicy chili, baked beans, potato salad, coleslaw, and sliced meats on toothpicks at them. By the time they reached the exit, Gaby couldn't have taken another bite.

Passing up an auction, they moved to the entertainment that included sad-faced clowns in miniature cars, unicycle-riding jugglers, sleek horses put through their paces, and Scottish dancers.

The Tilt-o-Whirl left Gaby dizzy, but a drink of strawberry pop settled her stomach, and it was off to the Ferris wheel. Though it wasn't very large, they could see all over the fairgrounds from the top. They rode the carousel twice, then went through the funhouse, where as she exited, a burst of air blew her skirt over her head to the delight of spectators. Wyatt, grinning, pretended to take a picture.

Everything had been perfect up to now. His hand, first on her back, then at her waist, seemed natural. No matter how it made her feel, on his part the touching was only designed to help them stay together in the crowd. Or was it?

His smile was ready and his laugh, genuine. But then they were confronted with the tunnel of love, where a huge heart-shaped sign showed couples wound in each other's arms, kissing, and Gaby felt uneasy.

It was only a carnival ride, she assured herself, and definitely not one conducive to romance. Still, she fought trepidation as he helped her into a boat that was so tiny, they were almost in each other's laps. His arm went around the back of the seat by necessity as they floated through flaps of the double doors into the darkness, with strains of "Moon River" coming at them from speakers along the way.

Other couples rode close after and before, giggles and squealed protests, then long silences indicating they were taking advantage of the ride's theme. Gaby was all too aware of Wyatt's mouth close to her ear. At this proximity the scent of his shaving lotion was intoxicating.

Maybe he would kiss her, if only for a lark. Her lips prickled with anticipation, but nothing happened, and they emerged, blinking against the blinding sun.

"I hope you noticed that I kept my promise," he muttered as he helped her out. "I didn't even nibble your ear."

"Your behavior was above reproach, sir," she sang, hiding her disappointment.

"It wasn't easy."

"I would have granted you amnesty," she said. "A kiss is obligatory in the tunnel of love."

He frowned. "I didn't know that."

"Move along," the ride attendant ordered.

"Want to go again and make things right?" Wyatt sounded as if he were playing along with a joke, but his eyes said otherwise.

"Yes," she agreed softly. Yes, yes, yes.

"Hey, you two. Been on the Comet?" Beau appeared between them suddenly and clapped a hand to each of their shoulders.

Gaby could have kicked him. "Not yet."

"It's a blast. Let's go. I'll sit in front, you two in the back."

"I think Gaby's had enough rides for one day." Wyatt's eyes didn't leave her face.

"Are you sure it's Gaby you're worried about, Uncle?" Beau laughed. "Not chicken, are you?"

"There you are." Ruth Ann came toward them at a skip. She wore a T-shirt with hot pink letters that said, "Meet me at the Fair." Her hair was pulled into a ponytail this time, but it still bounced with each of her steps. "Hi, Beau. Having a good time?" She didn't wait for an answer. "You're Gaby. I've been meaning to come by for an introduction. How are you bearing up?"

"She's doing fantastic," Beau said.

"How nice." The girl's eyes didn't reflect her twenty-four-tooth smile. Grasping Wyatt's elbow, she led him to one side. "Excuse us, you two, I need to talk to this guy for one minute."

The minute stretched to two, three, four. Beau began to fidget. "C'mon, Gaby," he pleaded. "Those two will be at it all night. Wyatt doesn't want to ride the Comet anyhow. He'll wait for us."

Not wanting to crush the boy's exuberance, Gaby agreed, though she would rather have remained for the promised boat ride, if it took an hour. As she feared, by the time the Comet came to a stop, Ruth Ann and Wyatt were gone.

"Ah-hah," Beau said, laughing. "He was waiting for a chance to get away. C'mon. Let's go again."

Was it true that Wyatt had been hoping for the right moment to escape?

After a while, Beau caught sight of some school chums and ran off to join them. Gaby strolled around the midway alone, listened to songs by a barbershop quartet, bought peanuts she didn't want, then abandoning all hope that Wyatt would come looking for her, went to view the quilts. Marianne's quilt hadn't won anything, but she was content with a second-prize ribbon for her green apple pie.

When Wyatt still hadn't appeared by the time Frank and Marianne were ready to go home, Gaby rode with them.

Nearly a week of unseasonable cold was followed by a sunny morning at last. Since their day at the fair, Wyatt hadn't hinted that he and Gaby had been more than employer and employee. Though they exchanged good mornings and an occasional smile, everything continued as before.

No more fences needed to be mended, but among other things, the hay had to be put in before it rained. Filling the silo was a horrendous job, and after Gaby's first ten minutes at it, with Wyatt as a no-nonsense partner, she understood why Marianne said she'd rather dig ditches.

Standing on metal rungs that ran up the side of the cylindrical-shaped structure, and scraping gook off heavy doors so they could close and lock was bad enough, but perching on the side of a tractor while Wyatt worked the blower was worse.

If she'd wished for hot weather before, now she wished it would go away. She was sweltering under the relentless sun. Not only did the noise not allow for conversation, hay kept blowing in her eyes, her nose, and ears. It found its way up the legs of her jeans, in her shoes, and under the neck of her shirt.

When they broke off for a sandwich, she was too uncomfortable to eat.

"You took off your mask again," Wyatt accused when she began coughing nonstop.

"I can't breathe with it on. What I need is earplugs. The decibels would be off the chart."

"If you'd do what I tell you to do, we'd get through faster."

"In other words," she retorted in kind, "when you say jump, I say how high?"

"You've got it. Otherwise you can go back and help Marianne in the kitchen."

"She doesn't need help," Gaby snarled, hurt that his attitude toward her hadn't changed one iota. "And I'm capable of following orders, Mr. Rafferty, sir."

Ignoring her sarcasm, he thrust the nose and mouth mask at her. "Let's see if you can."

The work was even more tedious than it had been before. Again and again the pipe clogged, and she had to shout for Wyatt to shut the machine off, so they could fix it. Then she got another fit of coughing and had to scream for him to stop again.

"What's wrong now?"

"Excuse me for choking."

"I told you to wear that mask." His expression was one of fury.

"Why do you hate me so much?"

"You believe I hate you because I don't turn to butter when you bat your eyelashes at me?"

She swallowed hard. "I thought we'd gone beyond that kind of accusation."

"In other words, you thought I was so completely under your spell, I'd tap dance to your tune?"

"You were different at the fair."

His laugh was an ugly growl. "We all have weak moments."

Swiping an arm across her eyes to clear her vision, she squinted up at him. "Meaning you consider behaving like a human being a weakness?"

"Meaning you have a face that tends to make a man forget the important things in life."

Was that meant to be a compliment? "Important things? In other words . . ."

He threw up his hands and snatched away her mask.

"That's it. There's no time for debate. We're working against the weather."

"So let's do it."

"Not a chance. You're a distraction."

"You need me."

"Like I need two extra thumbs. Get back to the house and make yourself useful. Send Beau out."

"Gladly." She jumped into the tractor, misstepping the first time and sliding to her knees awkwardly before getting into the seat. Saying all the angry things to herself she hadn't thought to say to Wyatt's face, she made a wide swing back to the house.

Too late, she saw the rock, swerved, and attempted to steer around it. Not reacting, the tractor lurched into a ravine and slid down, down until its wheel was wedged against a cut-off tree trunk.

Frantically, she worked her levers and her pedals, but no amount of maneuvering helped. "I might as well face the music," she muttered, jumping clear.

But no. Immediately she formulated a picture of the greeting she'd receive when she trudged back, oozing apologies. Instead, she crumpled to the ground and did nothing.

Expecting him to appear when the shadow fell across her path, she leapt to her feet, ready with an explanation.

"Problem, Sunshine?" Frank was wearing a plaid shirt and faded jeans, but as far as she was concerned it was a blue stretch suit with a red cape.

She gestured toward the tractor.

"How did it happen?"

"I'm so stupid."

"Stupid you're not"

"That isn't what your brother will say when he sees my predicament."

"Let's make sure he doesn't see it, then. Hold this." Frank handed her the hammer he'd been carrying and swung agilely into the driver's seat.

While he set to work making the monstrous machine rock back and forth, Gaby paced and watched for signs of Wyatt. "Hurry. Please."

The tractor roared, rocked forward, then sank again, and again. Swearing under his breath, Frank got out and contemplated the situation. Wedging a handy branch before and after the wheels, he climbed up again. This time when the machine jogged forward, it was free.

"I'll love you forever," she cried, sprinting over to hug her rescuer. "Nobody has to know about this, do they?"

"Wyatt, you mean?"

"Or your wife." Gaby raised her shoulders and lowered them. "Marianne believes I'm a total incompetent already."

"This'll be our little secret."

"I'd appreciate it." When she was at the controls again, he guided her with arm movements, until she was able to turn in the right direction.

''Way to go, Sunshine,'' he called after her.

Her tears had stopped, but still she thought of Wyatt's unfair attack. Why, she couldn't help wondering, couldn't he be more like his brother?

A visit to the doctor for Marianne gave Gaby a chance to see Burlington at last. It was busier than she'd expected it to be, and after Woodbridge, seemed like a whole candy store of bustling department stores and businesses. On an impulse, while waiting for Marianne, she bought a blue denim jumpsuit with a wide belt, picked up some graph paper, a how-to book on perspective, and drawing pencils in different degrees of softness.

Though she hadn't had an occasion in mind when she'd made the purchases, she was glad she had when she saw Marianne baking an applesauce cake with chocolate frosting. It was Beau's birthday, though nobody had bothered to tell her he'd turn sixteen that day.

The party was festive, with two of Beau's schoolmates, as well as June Weems. Though loud music wasn't a rule in the Rafferty house, it was allowed this time and Beau seemed pleased.

When his friends had gone, he scurried to his room with his loot, and Gaby wandered onto the porch. Wyatt followed shortly after, and she couldn't help but wonder if he would have ventured out if he'd known she was there.

''If this was my house,'' she told him, pretending

all was well between them, "this would be my favorite spot. After dinner, I'd stand right here and watch night spill over the pastures, the roofs, and the treetops."

Sliding his lower lip forward, he nodded. "Night brings peace to the land."

"City inhabitants haven't got a clue about what night really is."

"How do we manage to keep the secret?" he asked, playing along.

"Easy. There are too many competing lights—from cars, stores, streetlamps—for anyone to appreciate the moon. Too many sounds to hear the cry of owls or the call of nightbirds."

An owl hooted as if on cue, and Wyatt smiled down at her, wide and genuine this time, making her heart turn over. "Not that I'm a judge," she pushed on. "But June will be my favorite month in Vermont. The weather's warm, but not too warm. The air is sweeter. Leaves are greener, and everywhere I look, I see black-eyed susans, buttercups, and lilacs."

"I like October." Wyatt leaned with his elbows on the porch rail. "The leaves turn orange, red, and yellow. There's a nip in the air and the sky is so brilliant a blue it hurts your eyes."

"It sounds beautiful," she said, thinking, *I'll be here then, and maybe it'll be my favorite time of year, too.*

"Part of it is that I like handing out taffy and candy apples to the ghosts and witches that come around on Halloween."

"I love that, too, if I'm not dressing in costume and going to a party."

"You like parties as well as picnics?"

Was it a trick question? "I'd have a hard time choosing."

"I can only imagine how you'd look decked out as a princess." His eyes looked more deep set in the shadows. "You were born to wear fancy dresses."

Was he thinking of his mother, and her mania for new clothes? "Not so. Last Halloween I dressed as a computer."

He laughed. "How did you do that?"

"Easy." She gestured. "I put shoulder straps on a huge cardboard box, cut out a plastic window for my monitor, and fastened a keyboard to my middle."

"What a waste." His probing look caused a minor implosion of her senses, alerting her of a possible kiss and she steadied for it. This time, she didn't care what excuse he made for his actions—his astrology reading in the morning newspaper, or the position of Jupiter. Instead, he pushed off. "I'd better get going."

Where to? she wanted to ask but didn't, afraid he might revert to type and say it was none of her business. Besides, his destination didn't matter. She knew who his companion would be. Long after he'd backed the car down the driveway and disappeared, she stared at the road after him.

When she'd bathed, she read for a while, out of a sense of obligation to her mystery book, then watched an unfunny sitcom on television in spite of horizontal zigzags.

When it was over, she went to the kitchen for a glass of milk to drink while she wrote overdue letters to her mother, Kip, and to Dennis, asking him to send brochures on graphic arts programs here, in New York, and in surrounding states.

She'd just licked the last stamp and sealed the flap when headlights slid across the window. Crossing the room, she peered out and saw that there were two vehicles—one a station wagon with Ruth Ann at the wheel. She wore a yellow slicker and her long hair was stuffed in a yellow hat.

"Hi." The girl looked surprised. "We didn't think anyone would still be up. Especially you."

"Would you like coffee?" Gaby asked, forcing a hospitable tone.

"I'd kill for a cup." Ruth Ann sank into a chair. "What a night, huh, Wyatt?"

From the exchange Gaby heard as she measured out the coffee, the two had come back from a shift in a volunteer rescue squad that drove to the scene of accidents and fires to do what they could before ambulances and fire trucks could arrive.

That night their squad had administered first aid to a crash victim at "the Curve"—a loopy stretch famous in the county for accidents.

"After we stopped the bleeding," Ruth Ann went

on, "all we could do was pray for the paramedics. But they told us the woman will be fine."

"It sounds worthwhile." Gaby put coffee cups and spoons in front of the two. "I'd like to join the group."

"You'd have to take classes," the girl said with a supercilious smile, "and it's quite a course."

"I already know CPR."

Ruth Ann laughed. "A level head is the first prerequisite. From what I've heard, it's all you can do to milk a cow. Thanks for the coffee. I have to go."

"I'll walk you out, Ruthie," Wyatt offered.

Through the window, Gaby saw them silhouetted together. Then Wyatt opened the door of the station wagon, tucked the girl inside, and she drove away.

"Couldn't you sleep?" he asked, back again.

"I had letters to write."

He took the cups to the sink and rinsed them under the tap.

"Did you entertain everybody in this squad of yours with stories about my comical adventures, trying to play dairy farmer?"

"What's got your back up?"

"Not a thing," she snapped, gathering her letter-writing paraphernalia.

He barred her way. "Want to tell me about it?"

"So you can blab to 'Ruthie?' "

"How's that again?"

"You and your snide little friend walk around under this cone of superiority because you know how to stack hay in the silo, never giving a thought to the fact that I might know a few things you don't.''

''I didn't say that. Neither did Ruthie.''

''Yes, you did, in a dozen different ways.''

He grinned. ''You're jealous.''

''Why should I be?''

''That's what I'm wondering.''

''You're writing this scenario,'' she said, brushing past. ''If it makes you feel irresistible to believe that I care what you do, so be it.''

He caught her arm. ''One of these days, you're going to get what you're asking for.''

''What might that be?'' Her heart began to hammer, and before he could answer, she tore herself free and ran to her room.

It was much later, as she lay in bed glaring at the ceiling, that the truth struck. Wyatt was right. She wasn't angry because Ruth Ann poked fun at her. She was jealous.

Why would she be jealous unless—unless she was hopelessly in love with him?

Chapter Eight

Summer actually did come to Vermont, Gaby marveled. Over the next few days the outside thermometer registered over a hundred. Besides regular chores, daylight hours were taken up with a thorough cleaning of the milkroom in preparation for quarterly inspection.

Ron Jessup, the closest neighbor to the west, squat and balding, arrived with his manure spreader and helped with harrowing and seeding. When that was finished, Gaby, part of a three-tractor convoy, with Legs trotting behind as if the work couldn't be done without his supervision, headed to Jessup's farm to reciprocate.

Still smarting from Wyatt's smug remark about her jealousy and the realization that her feelings for him had gone too far, she nevertheless did as she was told and kept out of his way.

That seemed to suit him, as he'd made no overtures toward her either.

At five-fifteen every afternoon, it was also part of her routine to return to the barn, to travel down one aisle and another of just-milked cows, scooping a mixture of grain that smelled like molasses from a wheelbarrow to feeders in front of the waiting animals. This job she liked. Catching the sweet smell, the cows would toss their heads and moo enthusiastically at the prospect of this dessert. At least she was welcome in the barn.

"Phone call for you," Beau called as she was finishing up. "Dennis Laird."

"Yes, yes," she said, quickening her pace.

Hearing Dennis's voice was exactly what she needed to put her life in perspective. To remind her how much she liked her nightly runs along the beach, one-day sales at the department stores, and eating pepperoni pizza with him at her favorite sidewalk café.

Imagine talking to someone from a place where there were no cows, no silos, and best of all, no Wyatt.

"How did you get the phone number?"

"From information. Though you might have sent it along in your letter. Letter, singular. Given all the time you've been gone, I expected more."

"I've been too busy."

"I didn't want you to think I'd forgotten you, kiddo," he said, after relating a few tales about upcoming marriages and unfortunate separations of people they both knew. He'd been talking to someone at Lennox Ink, a company they'd discussed before she left, as being a perfect place for her to start. "The head honcho is in Philadelphia at the moment. I can't get word until he comes back, and I don't want to seem too eager."

"No, of course not."

"If it works, you can tell your uncle where to go."

"Have you found a loophole in the contract I signed?"

"I think so."

"Think isn't good enough. I need to get out of here."

"You sound like you're crying."

Was she? "You know me. I get weepy over movie previews. However, you'd be crying, too, if you had to work for the guy I work for."

"Anybody who could be mean to you must be Atilla the Hun."

"He makes Atilla the Hun look like a pussycat. Oh, Dennis, hurry. I'm counting on you."

"Love you, kiddo," he said, as he always did, not only to her, but to everybody, when he said good-bye.

"Love you, too."

She'd been so engrossed in pleading, she hadn't heard Wyatt come in. He was behind her glaring at papers he'd taken out of the file cabinet.

"Still looking for a loophole?" he commented, not glancing up from his task.

How much had he heard? "I didn't think even you would eavesdrop on a private conversation."

"Private? You were wailing so loud, I thought you wanted everybody to hear. I needed these papers."

"I'll bet you did."

He raised an eyebrow. "Why would I have the remotest interest in anything you have to say to your friend?''

''Couldn't you have waited until I was finished talking?''

''How did I know how long the hugs and kisses would go on? The feed man is here, and I need to check over last month's bills with him.''

Not trusting herself to say more, she swept past him, through the back door, across the field, and down the road, not caring where she was going, except that it was out of his sphere of influence.

Up one hill she walked, and down another, until she was breathless. Then she sat under a low dipping willow, watched a pair of chipmunks cavorting in the branches above, and listened to the lament of a pee wee, as she tried to clear her mind.

Dennis had spoken of a possible way out of her agreement with Uncle Arnold. He had also mentioned a job at a choice company. If it came through, she might be sitting at a desk in the city two weeks from now.

Is that what you want? a small voice whispered in her ear. *Is that truly what you want?*

Though it had been warm when she'd settled under the tree to feel sorry for herself, a breeze came up suddenly, and now she felt chilly. Who needed weather a person couldn't depend on?

She'd almost reached the house, when she stopped walking. Across the meadow, she spotted Cleo, the favorite Rafferty milker, cantering toward her as if expecting a hearty welcome. How had the frisky little cow managed to escape?

Fearing the worst, Gaby wrenched her attention to the gate. Ohmigosh. When she'd left in a huff, she hadn't locked it. The animal must have nosed it open. What was she going to do?

Not wanting to alert the others and invite more disdain, she tried coaxing, then scolding. Neither worked. It was as if Cleo were playing with her. She'd allow Gaby to get close, only to scramble toward the woods.

What if there was a deadfall in that section where the animal was headed? Frank had said something earlier about a fallen tree that needed cutting and hauling.

She hated to take a chance, but having no choice, she made a dash for the barn where she grabbed a rope and quickly filled a bucket with cow candy. So far, so good. Back she raced again, and her heart sank like a stone when she didn't see the escapee.

"Cleo. Here girl. Nice girl. I have something for you," she tried. Cleo didn't respond.

She was about to return to the house and confess her latest sin when the animal appeared at the edge of the trees. Cleo had spotted the bucket, and her appetite was getting the better of her. She sped toward it, and miraculously Gaby was able to get the rope around her neck.

In answer to her fervent prayer, she circled the shed,

got Cleo penned without being seen, and all before the dinner bell sounded.

Though she allowed herself a few moments, leaning against the side of the barn to ease a stitch in her side, she was out of breath when she reached the porch. Though she'd been careless for leaving the gate open, she was proud of herself for handling the situation. This time Frank hadn't even had to come to her rescue.

"Where have you been?" Wyatt asked, meeting her at the door.

"I went for a walk." Realizing how disheveled she must look, she nevertheless held her head high. "So shoot me."

"Don't tempt me," he muttered.

The meal was delicious as usual, with pot roast and potato pancakes. Gaby's frantic activity had left her ravenous, though she hadn't realized how enthusiastically she was eating until she noticed Wyatt staring at her in surprise. Smiling to herself, she slowed down.

Marianne was about to dish out blackberry pie when three hard knocks sounded at the door.

"Expecting anybody?" Frank asked. When no one answered, he scraped back his chair.

"Rafferty. All o' you. Get moving quick." Ron Jessup burst in, took off his knit cap, and scratched his bald spot. "I got trouble. You got trouble."

"What's wrong?" Instantly Wyatt was on his feet.

"A bunch of your animals got theirselves in my orchard, that's what's wrong."

"How?" Marianne wanted to know.

"Who cares how? They tore through the yard first." He jabbed a thumb toward the door. "Then they trampled my wife's vegetable garden."

"How many cows are we talking about?"

"Six or seven, as I could see. Could be more in the thicket."

Frank pressed his lips together and blew. "We'll take care of it."

"Ah yup. You better. The wife's turning the air blue saying words I never heard her say before."

"Everybody's on call here." Wyatt singled Gaby out as if he thought she'd try to hang back. "Everybody."

"There must be a broken spot we didn't notice in the fence," Frank said.

"I checked, like you said," Beau argued.

"Apparently you didn't check good enough."

"Why am I always the guilty one?"

"It was my fault," Gaby admitted, not able to let Beau take the blame.

Five pairs of eyes fastened on her as she gave an abbreviated version of how she hadn't latched the gate, and Cleo had escaped. "I caught her, so I assumed it was all right."

"Why didn't you tell us before the damage was done?" Wyatt's expression was Dantean.

"I thought it was only Cleo."

"You should have realized the rest would go, too."

"I need to get over to Matt's house," Beau complained. "I promised to help with that airplane model."

"Afterward," Frank said. "There have to be enough of us to surround the strays when we spot 'em."

"*Afterward* could take all night and the best part of the next two days," Beau argued.

"Let's find those cows," Wyatt said, not listening.

"I'm sorry about your wife's garden," Gaby told Jessup, who was the last to leave. "I'll put it right."

"How? There was inches of green shoots up already, and she was talking about canning."

"We'll get the animals first," Frank told him. "The garden comes later."

"Tell that to my Elsie," Jessup grumbled.

Luck was with them and in less than two hours, a head count verified that only one animal was still gone.

"It's Dilly," Beau said. "You know how ornery she is. She's dug in somewhere laughing at us."

Gaby and Beau were dismissed, while Frank, Wyatt, and some helpful neighbors continued the search in the growing darkness. By a little after nine, it was over. Dilly was where she belonged. When the men came inside wearily, Marianne poured coffee and dished out pie.

"None for me, thanks." Gaby felt too embarrassed to sit in their midst and experience their displeasure.

Frank pulled out a chair and insisted that she join them at the table. "Don't look so stricken, Sunshine. It happens to the best of us."

Not to Wyatt, she thought miserably, as the others traded stories about other times they'd had to round up lost cows. Not all their tales had a happy ending.

"You should have said something right off," Marianne berated her later when they were alone with the dishes. "Common sense should have told you cows follow the leader."

"I should have said something. But I didn't." Tired of hearing about it, Gaby met the woman's glare straight on, and Marianne actually looked away first.

"Today we make ice cream," Bridget sang the following morning when Gaby came in. "Wild strawberry. Wait till you taste it."

Still depressed about her latest escapade, Gaby had trouble concentrating, though recipe directions were clearly printed on a card.

"I never mind this part of the job," Bridget said when they opened the container with only a partly frozen mixture to add the flavorings. "Customers drive from farther away than you'd believe. Can't get stuff this good in the supermarkets."

"It smells delicious." Gaby sniffed.

"We'll each have a big bowl when we finish. Nobody minds. That's why I have a weight problem." Bridget patted her ample hips. "I heard some of the cows got out last night."

"Guess who forgot to latch the gate?"

Bridget slapped at the air. "Forget it. I could tell you stories about what happens with newcomers."

"Tell that to Wyatt. He's such a stone-face."

"He's not so bad, all things considered." Bridget began fitting the tops back on the containers. "Be grateful he isn't like his brother."

"Pete Rafferty was difficult?" If so, Gaby counted herself fortunate that he was gone.

The woman's eyes widened. "Of course not. Pete was a doll. I'm talking about Frank. I couldn't take two of him, could you?"

"Why do you say that?" Gaby asked, puzzled.

"Poor Marianne, having to put up with his shenanigans all the time. Don't tell me he hasn't tried his line on you yet."

"He's only being friendly."

"Hah! A little too friendly. The last time he cornered me on the path as I walked home, I told him in no uncertain terms I'd blacken his eye if he didn't keep his distance."

"It's hard to believe," Gaby said, still thinking there must be a mistake.

"He's going slow with you because you're new. But take my advice and never let him get you alone. He's a born flirt."

Gaby didn't ask any more questions about what Bridget had told her, but she couldn't help thinking about it after lunch as she rolled the wheelbarrow filled with replacement plants over to the Jessup house.

Frank Rafferty? Impossible.

As she weeded, dug, and hoed, she hardly listened to Elsie Jessup rave on and on about her ruined vegetable patch, as if it would have earned the cover of a garden magazine if it hadn't been trampled. Periodically, Gaby uttered another apology and before she left, Elsie's anger had evaporated.

''Come back soon,'' the woman called. ''We'll have tea. I hear you're a tea drinker, too.''

Bridget wouldn't lie, Gaby thought, after offering a vague acceptance of the woman's invitation. Sensible as she seemed, Bridget could have been one of those women who believe every man who looks in her direction is flirting.

After her shower that night, Gaby read a bit. She was finally on the last chapter, but didn't care in the slightest who the murderer was. It was only for the sense of completion it gave her to turn the last page.

Hungry for a snack, she went to the kitchen for another slice of pie. As she passed Wyatt's office, she paused to take a sip of milk. A strip of light shone under the door. He was working late again.

Was he ever distracted by thoughts of her? Did she charge recklessly through his dreams? Probably not. When Dennis came through for her and she left Rafferty Farms forever, would Wyatt miss her, or would he celebrate? She swallowed a bitter ache at the back of her throat.

She was still standing there when the door flew open.

"Why aren't you in bed?" Wyatt's hair was fetchingly tousled, as if he'd run his fingers through it while he worked the adding machine. "You've got tractor duty in the morning."

"I read the schedule," she threw at him, made especially belligerent by the thoughts she'd been having about him before he appeared. "I've been doing a good job, even if you don't say it."

"Except when you leave the gate open."

"Am I ever going to live that down? It can't possibly be that I'm a disappointment to you."

"Why do you say that?"

"Because you didn't expect anything of me when I arrived."

He waited, as if he knew she'd say more.

"If you're tired of having me around, send me home." She threw one arm out to the side in a wide gesture.

His mouth worked in self-censorship. "You'd like that, wouldn't you?"

"Under the circumstances, what do you think?"

"Gaby," he called softly as she turned away.

"What is it?" Her heart picked up a beat as she wondered if he was having second thoughts.

"You have a milk mustache," he said, then went back into his office and closed the door.

Chapter Nine

Still irritable, Marianne barely spoke when Gaby came to help with the next day's lunch preparations. Part of her problem was that she'd have to continue wearing a modified cast a bit longer. Part, but not all.

Pretending not to notice, Gaby kept up a cheery patter—remarking on the weather and sympathizing with the woman's dashed hopes for returning to a normal routine.

"Maybe I should try crying to get the doctor to change his mind." Marianne leaned forward to knead the biscuit dough. "It works for you."

"What do you mean?" Gaby knew exactly what the woman meant. But she needed to hear her say it.

"When things get rough, *you* shed a tear, and the men back off. Like when you let the cows out."

"You think I cry intentionally?" That did it. Gaby pulled out a chair and sat down. "What have I done to make you resent me, Marianne?"

"Not a thing."

"Can't we be honest with each other?"

The woman's eyes flashed, and she continued kneading with more gusto than she had before. ''You don't belong here.''

At least it was out in the open. ''I used to think I didn't,'' Gaby said. ''Now I'm not so sure.''

''Because of Wyatt?''

''Don't be silly.''

''A minute ago you called for honesty.''

Was she so obvious? ''Because of a lot of things.''

''But Wyatt is the biggest part of it.''

Gaby's gaze slid to the window and beyond, where Wyatt was talking to the vet. The man wore a red knit sweater with reindeers across the chest. Periodically, he shuffled his feet and spat. ''Maybe I shouldn't answer that question.''

''Then you already have.'' Marianne formed the dough into a smooth ball and began pressing it into a rectangle. ''Has anyone told you about Pete?''

''Only that he lives in Upstate New York and works for a hardware conglomerate. He's married and has twin daughters.'' Gaby had gleaned that much information from Bridget.

''You haven't wondered why he isn't here?''

''I assume he preferred working in the city.''

''It wasn't Pete. It was Rolly, his wife. She was one of those tourists who swarm over Vermont all summer and fall, instantly in love with the land. She fell in love with Pete, too. She looked cute in overalls and saw a way to avoid routine, air pollution, and feuding family members.''

''It sounds like Priscilla Rafferty all over again.''

''You know about Priscilla?'' Surprised, Marianne looked up from her work. ''Yes. I guess you would. People still talk about it, even though she left a long time ago.''

''What happened with Pete and Rolly?''

''After the wedding, the men used their free time to build a house for the new couple,'' Marianne went on. ''So they could have the privacy newlyweds need. You've seen it, through the trees on the other side of the road.''

Gaby nodded. ''I wondered why it was vacant. It's almost finished, isn't it?''

''Almost. The two of them planned the size and placement of the rooms together, and Rolly was bubbling over about how she'd be living in a house no one had ever lived in before.''

''What happened?''

''It took less than a year for her love to turn to hate. She missed shopping and the theater. Suddenly she hated not seeing her mother and father on the weekends. She couldn't understand why anybody would want to spend twelve hours a day doing something that has to be done all over the next day, and the day after that. She gave Pete a choice. The farm or her.''

''He chose her.''

Marianne shrugged. ''He was in love.''

"Is the marriage working out?"

"He still kisses the ground she walks on. But they came back for Christmas, and he admitted that he hates the posturing necessary to keep moving up the company ladder. He hates traffic, and neighbors so close he's forced to listen to their choice in music whether he likes it or not. But he wouldn't fit in here anymore either."

"And you believe I could influence Wyatt to do the same thing?"

"This whole operation would be dumped in our laps—Frank's and mine. We can't handle it alone. It started as a family enterprise and was meant to stay that way."

Gaby stared at the stuffed cow in the alcove. "Wyatt resents me more than you do. Even if he didn't, I could never convince him to desert the farm."

"But you'd try."

Would she? "I truly can't answer that."

"Let me put it this way." Marianne stopped working. "Do you see yourself milking cows for the rest of your life?"

"No," Gaby admitted, the truth scratching at a sensitive spot in her reasoning. "I worked too hard to get where I am."

"So you see, the sooner you're gone, the better off everybody will be." Marianne fluttered a hand toward the over-sink cabinet as if the conversation was at an end. "Get me a baking sheet, will you? Then sound the dinner bell."

What the woman said made sense, Gaby had to admit as she watched the Rafferty men file in—Frank looking like anything but the Don Juan Bridget accused him of being, as he and his son boxed playfully.

Gaby had mastered many tasks, but she wasn't a dairy farmer and never could be.

Even for Wyatt? a small voice echoed inside her head, and she had to laugh. So far, he hadn't even suggested she make the sacrifice. So why was she wasting energy on a zero possibility?

Wash day started early. So the next morning, at the breakfast table, Gaby set to work, spotting stains, mending and matching socks, while the elderly machine chugged away.

Why didn't they use a dryer? she grumbled as she hung the resulting wash. The family had a VCR and a computer. They even had computer games. Why would a dryer be considered too citified?

When cold weather set in, if she was still here, she'd remark casually about long underwear frozen in grotesque positions on the lines. By then she might be in good graces enough to get a civil answer, though she wouldn't count on it.

When the clotheslines were sagging with the last load, she decided to take advantage of the beautiful day and make use of the pond. On an impulse, after she'd donned her swimming suit, she stopped at the kitchen door with a beach towel slung over one shoulder. "Want to come along?" she asked Marianne.

The woman grunted. "You know I can't go in the water."

"You could sit on the sidelines and enjoy a change of scenery. Watch the squirrels and listen to the bobolinks."

"This scenery suits me fine. There are pies to be baked."

"Can I do anything?"

"Nothing." The woman smiled. "Have a good time."

Was she hearing things? Gaby wondered. Maybe the talk she'd had with Marianne had helped.

As she was picking her way down the path, bordered by Johnny-jump-ups and dandelions, she saw him and slowed, wanting to give her pulse a chance to resume its normal beat. Wyatt was sitting with his back to the trunk of a beech tree, taking his time with a sack lunch Marianne had prepared.

"Ah-hah!" Gaby pointed a finger at him. "Caught in the act."

"Ah-hah?" he questioned.

"I see you don't have anything against picnics in general. As long as they aren't called 'picnics.' "

"The word implies more than just eating." His smile was closed-mouthed.

"You're right. It conjures up visions of—" She

gave an exaggerated shudder. "Things like people laughing and enjoying themselves."

"Okay," he said jovially. "Enough."

"I finished the laundry early, so I thought I'd try the water."

"You're entitled."

She was glad to hear she was entitled to something.

"Polka dots." He chuckled under his breath. "Couldn't you have found a skimpier suit?"

"They didn't have any of those eighteen-ninety numbers with knee-length bloomers and a matching elastic bathing cap in the malls back home."

"How about something in between?"

"When I swim, I like to swim. I don't want bulky fabric weighing me down." Why was she explaining to him?

"People who swim in earnest usually settle on a one-piece suit."

"I don't plan to swim the Channel. Just to enjoy myself."

"Go ahead. Don't mind me."

Don't mind him? He had to be joking. She would have felt more at ease performing at a five-thousand-spectator water ballet.

"Care to join me?" Though she knew what his answer would be, she felt called upon to ask.

"I don't have time to swim."

He sounded as if he would have liked to plunge in, and why not? He could be so straight-backed at times she tended to forget he was human. "Meaning you don't take time?"

"Meaning what I said."

"I've been wanting to try this pond since I saw it."

"Better do it then, before winter sets in."

She looked up at the sky. "I imagine we'll have a dozen warm days before that."

"Don't depend on it."

"I've learned not to depend on anything," she countered. After laying her towel across a handy tree stump, she went over and stuck her foot in the water. Immediately she shrieked, and she pulled it out again.

Wyatt's laugh was an appreciative whoop. "I could have told you it's cold."

She frowned. "Ponds are supposed to be warm."

"Too many trees to allow the sun to do its job." He plucked an apple from his brown bag and polished it on his shirtfront.

"Can't take it?"

She shot him a defiant look, steadied herself, and plunged in. Feeling his eyes on her, she knifed through the water, then floated in and around cattails and water lilies, ignoring the cold with supreme effort.

"Not like a swimming pool back home, is it?"

"It's fine, once you get used to it." Not that she planned on that happening today.

When she'd stayed submerged long enough to satisfy his dare, she climbed out, bundled up in her towel, and sank on the grass beside him.

"Hey," he objected. "You're getting me wet."

"Can't take it?"

His answer was to finish his apple and drop the core in the bag with his sandwich wrappings. "I'd better get back to work."

She sits down, and he skitters away? Who was afraid of *whom*?

Without thinking, she caught his sleeve. "Stay. Frank said you hurry through your chores to leave time for pleasure."

"I do." A ray of sunshine stabbed through the canopy of leaves overhead and turned his eyes as luminous a green as ocean waves across warm sands.

"Show me," she said, his companionable tone filling her with new audacity.

He fought back a smile. "How do I do that?"

"Would there be anything wrong with you lying on the grass for half an hour, relaxing?"

"Yes, there would be." He reached over and adjusted the towel that had slipped off one of her shoulders and her face prickled with as much heat as if she'd stood in front of a blast furnace.

"The farm would fall to ruin?"

"It might."

"How?"

"One thing would lead to another."

"You're impossible." She settled back with an air of nonchalance she didn't feel. "I can't fault you for driving the rest of us, considering how you drive yourself.''

In the distance a dog was barking. It sounded like Legs. A tractor on the Jessup farm started up, stopped, and started again.

''You think I stayed here watching you swim only to take a breather from my work?'' Wyatt asked after a few minutes of silence.

She searched his face for a clue as to what he meant. ''Why not? The way you were going at that log with a chain saw, I'd think you could use a breather.''

He shook his head. ''You know why I'm still here, and it wasn't to finish my lunch.''

Her lips felt as dry as twigs. ''No?''

''No.'' Slowly, as if he hoped she would stop him, he leaned toward her, closer and closer.

As he dipped his head, she garnered all her effort and slid a trembling hand between his mouth and hers. ''Are you planning to kiss me?''

He waited until she'd moved her hand away, allowing his eyes to caress the lips he hadn't yet claimed. ''Unless you're holding me to the promise I made at Hill House.''

''No,'' she said, too quickly.

''I didn't think so.''

Again her hand moved between his lips and hers. ''You want to kiss me because you think I need to feel appreciated?''

A twitching at the corner of his mouth made an answer unnecessary. "What do you think?"

She swallowed hard. "I can only judge by reasons you've given me for kisses in the past."

"Kisses in the past," he muttered. "It has a poetic sound."

"There's nothing poetic about being humiliated." She tensed, afraid she'd pushed too hard. He'd hurl another painful remark at her, spring to his feet and stalk off.

Instead, he yanked the towel off her shoulders. "You want to know why?"

She inhaled sharply and nodded.

"Because you drive me crazy, and you know it." He sounded resentful. "Even under ordinary circumstances, when you're wearing baggy pants, with hay tangled in your hair and dirt on your face. But when you come at me wearing something that doesn't leave much to the imagination, I realize I'm not as strong as I thought I was."

"I'm not out to drive anybody crazy," she said, wondering why he always had to counter his motives with accusation.

"No?" He shifted his weight, putting himself in a position of command, and meeting no opposition this time, kissed her mouth until she had no choice but to kiss him back.

All the while his hands moved at her back, pressing, stroking, making her feel as if only the two of them existed in this special world he was creating. As if under his pose of perfect control stood a storybook hero who could perform every bit of magic she would ever need in her life. The thought staggered her.

"No man could hold out against your kind of attack," he whispered. "Seeing you like this, feeling your lips willing under mine, knowing we can never..."

This was his most maddening habit, she thought, wanting to wrap her arms around his neck, and rake his mouth to hers again. Since they'd met, time after time, he broke off without finishing strategic sentences.

If we don't become to each other what you'd like to become, it'll be your doing, Wyatt Rafferty, she wanted to say.

"If we stay here, I won't be responsible for what happens."

"I'll take my chances," she murmured.

"You'd like me to give in, wouldn't you?" He stopped moving, except for his mouth.

"Yes," she admitted.

"Who's this Dennis Laird who calls you?" The timbre of his voice had changed.

"A longtime friend. We work together."

He leaned back to study her face. "You go on dates with him, too?"

She didn't know if she could call their outings dates. "Yes."

"He kisses you good night?"

"Yes," she said, though after the kisses she'd exchanged with Wyatt, she wasn't sure Dennis's could be considered kisses.

He was pulling away emotionally as well as physically, she thought, experiencing a moment of panic. The shining moment was over.

"In other words, when you're not near the one you love, you make do with whoever's near," he said.

She fought the impulse to snap an answer back at him. It would be playing his game.

"It's hard to believe a man could maintain distance from you when you work together closely."

"Hard to believe or not, it's true."

"Well, it's back to work for me," he said, unfolding to a standing position.

"Right," she said, trying not to feel abandoned. "Hurry. You have to make up for lost time."

"Are you coming?" He held out his hand to her.

After a long moment of contemplating a grasshopper, who at the same time seemed to be contemplating her, she shook her head. "I'm going in the water again."

"Watch out for the bullfrogs."

"Let them watch out for me."

With a rueful smile, he wadded up his sandwich wrappings and left. Soon she heard the buzz of his saw.

Chapter Ten

Another trip to Burlington came unexpectedly when Beau broke his wrist playing softball. He protested vehemently that he didn't need his mother, but Marianne insisted on going along, and Gaby had to drive.

While they were alone in the waiting room, Gaby jumped at the chance to talk. "Have you ever worn your hair short?"

"My hair is straight as a stick. It wouldn't curl around my cheekbones the way yours does." Marianne flashed Gaby a knowing look. "A haircut won't keep Frank from flirting with every female in sight, if that's what this sudden interest in my appearance is about."

"I didn't mean . . ."

"Yes, you did. But I can assure you, gold mascara won't do the trick. Or lipsticks with names like Honey Spice and Ripe Melon."

She might not have fooled Marianne. Still she couldn't back off. "Why put up with it?"

"Frank is Frank. He likes women, so he plays games. It doesn't mean anything."

"It can't be much fun for you."

"I think he does it because deep down inside, he

149

holds himself responsible for his mother's leaving. One of those 'If-I'd-been-a-better-kid-she-would-have-stayed' kind of things. Naturally, Wyatt got all the sympathy. He was the baby. Frank was sixteen and didn't need a mother—or so everybody thought. But he was crushed, too.''

''You're saying he only wants everybody to like him?'' In Gaby's opinion, Marianne's excuse for her husband's thoughtless behavior was stretching understanding too far.

''Frank and I got married way too young.'' Marianne clasped her hands together in her lap. ''He didn't have a chance to 'sow his wild oats,' as they say.''

''Neither did you.''

''That doesn't matter to a woman.''

''If a woman doesn't date other men, how does she know she's in love?'' Gaby asked.

''I knew. I never loved anyone but Frank since I was old enough to know there was such a thing as love, and I never will. I never had crushes on rock singers or movie stars like other girls did. Even after all these years, I look at him while he's sleeping and think how lucky I am.''

''Except that he embarrasses you.''

''Sometimes,'' Marianne admitted. ''Other people think he means it. You thought so, too, didn't you?''

Gaby's smile was tentative. ''To be honest, I didn't know he was doing it. I thought he was being friendly until . . .'' She didn't want to mention Bridget and get the woman in trouble.

"People talk, don't they?" Marianne sighed.

"Sit Frank down and explain that it bothers you."

"Can I expect him to be somebody he isn't? It's different with you. Besides being intelligent, you're gorgeous. Everything a man could want in a woman."

"Hardly that." Gaby didn't know how to respond.

"Enough." The woman picked up a handy magazine and began thumbing through the pages. "I'm not a glamour girl and I never will be."

Though the conversation ended there, Gaby felt encouraged. Marianne refused to go to a beauty salon for a professional cut while they were in the city. But when they got home, she allowed Gaby to snip off a few inches, then a few more, and a few more. The result was rewarding.

Marianne gasped in obvious pleasure when she saw herself in the hand mirror. "Frank will kill me."

"I think he'll like it. Actually there is some curl, without the length weighing it down."

Marianne put the mirror down. "If you're planning a makeover, forget it. The haircut is as far as I go."

Gaby was about to try a little more wheedling, at least enough to be allowed to pluck the woman's too-heavy eyebrows, when Beau called her from the other room. "Telephone. It's that man again."

"Did you get the packet I sent?" Dennis asked when she came on the line. "It should get there today."

"I haven't seen the mail today."

"Hang in there, kiddo. Things are coming together at Lennox. It looks good for you."

"I'm in no hurry."

Dennis was quiet for a long moment. "You aren't beginning to think of yourself as a Vermont Maid, are you?"

"Maybe I am," she admitted, realizing that it had been quite a while since she'd marked X's on her calendar.

"Hmm. How old is this young man who's interested in graphic art?"

"Sixteen."

"Then I assume he's not the one who's beating my time."

Dennis sounded as if he were only half kidding.

"Nobody's beating your time."

"It wouldn't work, babe. City Mouse, Country Mouse. You've heard the story."

"If it was only geography," she said softly, to herself as much as to him. "The bottom line is—he doesn't like me very much."

"This is worse than I thought. What about your ambitions? You planning to plow them under?"

Would she? Could she?

"Are you planning to move there permanently? Tell me before I put more time on this thing with Lennox."

"Nobody's asked me to stay." On Wyatt's desk was a letter from a seed company. As he talked on the phone earlier, he'd drawn a stick figure, garbed in a skirt. The character's hair was squiggly and it wore an angry face. She smoothed a hand across the paper. Was this doodle supposed to represent her? ''I have to go now.''

''If there's anything I can do.''

''You already have.''

''This guy is a fool.''

''Good-bye, Dennis.''

Going over the conversation in her mind, she went out to collect the mail. A bulky packet wound several times around with metallic tape was the material Dennis had promised to send. She'd teased him often about his wrapping style, saying the recipient would need a hand grenade to open it.

''This is great,'' Beau said when she handed it to him, immediately going at the tape with a paper knife. ''Thanks.''

''Happy reading. I think you'll find that you have a lot of options.''

City Mouse, Country Mouse, Dennis had said.

Okay, Gaby mused that night as she clicked off the light and closed her eyes, hoping to fall asleep immediately without a long session of what's and what-if's. She'd already admitted to herself that she loved Wyatt. What could she do about it? She honestly didn't know.

According to Bridget, Cole Rafferty had married the wrong girl. He, as well as his children, had suffered for it. Pete had done the same thing, to please Rolly.

Now he didn't fit anywhere. Would it be that way with her?

When she drifted off, she found herself at Hill House, except that in her dream, it was new, freshly painted, and sitting in a field of daffodils. She was standing on the porch, wearing a dress with a skirt that billowed in the breezes. Wyatt was beside her, telling her she was beautiful.

A knock-knock-knocking at her door stabbed through her subconscious, and she fought desperately to hold on to her dream. "Gaby, wake up."

"Oh, come on," she protested. "My head barely touched the pillow. It can't be time to get up."

The door opened and Beau looked in. "Sorry, but there's a fire at the Tierney place. Mom and I need to go, but she doesn't trust me to drive with my bandage."

Groaning, Gaby threw back the covers, staggered over, and looked out the window. The smell of smoke was strong even at this distance, and the sky was a sickly greenish orange. "Are you sure we should go?"

"They need all the help they can get. Wyatt and Frank have already gone. We'll take the camper."

From everything Gaby had been taught, firemen preferred that spectators stay away. But maybe it was different in Woodbridge.

At Marianne's direction, she put cold beer and soft drinks in the back of the camper, then gathered up all available blankets and sweaters in case somebody needed protection against the chill. In less than fifteen minutes they were on the road. Five minutes after that, they pulled into a clearing some distance from a burning barn, where she got out and helped Marianne with her crutches.

Gaby hadn't known there were so many people in the area, though the haze of smoke, sparks, and burning debris would have kept her from recognizing many. Besides the firefighters, men, women, and teenagers were tearing in and out of the house, carrying boxes, furniture, and other valuables to safety in case the flames won the battle. Others led frightened animals from the blaze. Everybody seemed to be shouting directions to everybody else at the tops of their lungs.

The barn was a lost cause. Most attention was turned to saving the two-story frame house. A gray-haired woman stood off to one side, shivering in spite of the crocheted stole she wore around her shoulders. Gaby gathered that it was her son's farm.

"How did it start?" Gaby whispered.

"Hay," the woman said. "Heat had probably been building up in the stacks long before the flames broke out."

"The hay can start burning all by itself?"

"What does it matter how it started?" someone said. "The thing is to stop it."

"Where's Frank?" Marianne stretched herself taller to see over the milling crowd.

"Trying to get the animals free," the Tierney

woman said. ''The poor, poor things. My husband, too.''

Marianne sucked in her breath. ''You don't mean they're still inside!''

''My stars.'' An elderly man high-stepped over to them. ''The roof's going to go any minute.''

''What's taking them so long?'' Marianne anguished. ''Why don't they get out while they can?''

''Something could be wrong. Wait.''

''Here they come,'' Mrs. Tierney pointed as half a dozen bawling cows broke through the door that still hung partly on its hinges. A knot of men followed. One was Frank.

''Over here,'' Marianne beckoned for him.

Shading his eyes, he loped over, coughing hard. Working hard to get a good breath, he leaned forward with his hands on his knees. ''It was close, I'll tell you. A couple of rafters gave way, crashed down, and pinned some of the cows down.''

''Where's Hank?'' Mrs. Tierney asked fearfully. ''Where's my son?''

''Isn't he here?'' Frank asked.

Gaby curled her hands into tight fists. ''What about Wyatt?''

''The two of them were right behind me.'' Frank looked around, confused. ''At least they were. Hey, Bennington, have you seen my brother?''

The man shrugged.

Grim-faced, Frank pulled out of his wife's grasp. "I have to go back."

"No." Marianne snatched at him, but he broke away.

Another man tore after him, but before they reached the barn, there was a thunderous crash. Orange flames rose, and the roof collapsed. A woman screamed.

Gaby couldn't get a breath. She was still dreaming. That was it. She'd been thinking about Hill House, and in a minute, she'd wake up.

Except no dream could be so vivid.

Then off to the side, through the smoke, something moved. Another cow trotted to safety and two men followed, half running and half stumbling. Gaby spotted a glimpse of the green-and-black wool squares that made up Wyatt's work jacket, and cried out.

"Here they come," Marianne said numbly.

Mechanically, Gaby started forward, planning to wrap her arms around him and hold on until somebody pulled her off. Ruth Ann got there first. Gaby hadn't noticed her in the crowd, in spite of her yellow slicker. The girl was on tiptoe, kissing Wyatt's face.

"Did you get all the cows out?" someone asked.

"We did." Wearily he limped over, with Ruth Ann still clinging to his arm. "But it's gonna be a devil rounding 'em up."

"Get at it while you got the manpower," the old man said. "If you don't watch, the crowd'll break up."

Unable to contain tears of relief and not wanting to

make a spectacle of herself, Gaby hurled herself down the embankment to the camper. Closing herself in, she threw herself on the cot without turning on the light and wept.

Shouts and footsteps merged and became a roar, until she almost forgot where she was and whether it was day or night. Her former worries seemed meaningless. How differently this night might have ended.

When the door creaked open, the camper dipped with someone's weight. She sat up quickly and wiped her eyes with the back of her hand.

"I thought you only cried when you were mad," Wyatt drawled.

"I *am* mad. Don't ever do that again."

He grinned, his teeth white against his smoke-streaked skin. "I won't if I can help it."

"You just . . ." Searching for words, she flung one arm out to the side. "Just ran into the flames."

"Not exactly accurate. Did I need your permission?"

"If something had happened to you—" She broke off, not wanting to deal with another of his taunting comments if she left herself unprotected.

"If something happened to me—what?" He drew her to her feet.

"I came in here to be alone," she said, hating the tears she couldn't stop.

"So you could cry?"

"If it's any of your business." Noticing an angry red gash on his chin, she bit her lower lip.

"You want me to leave?" A corner of his mouth quivered as it lifted a fraction with an uncompleted smile.

She didn't need this. Any of it. Not windstorms, never-ending tasks, and accusations that made her feel powerless. Yes, she wanted him to leave.

Instead of telling him that, as if a button had been pushed to set her in motion, she wound her arms around his neck, pulled his face down to hers, and pressed her lips to his eyelids, his nose, his cheekbones, and the sides of his neck.

"Hey, you're getting soot all over your face," he said, laughing. "What's this about?"

"I'm glad you're safe."

"Apparently." He moved his hands up and down the sides of her rib cage.

"What were you thinking? What would have happened to the farm if you weren't there to hold it together?"

He brushed his mouth across the top of her head. "You were only thinking about the farm?"

"Yes," she answered too quickly. "No. I mean, naturally, I wouldn't want you to be hurt either."

"Naturally."

"We've lived under the same roof. Or even if we hadn't. Even if you were someone I didn't know. A storekeeper. A stranger I'd passed on the street. I wouldn't want him—you—to be . . .'' She knew she was rambling as the words flowed out; still she couldn't stop them.

''I get the picture,'' he interrupted, burrowing his face in the silkiness of her hair.

''Not that you aren't more important to me than a stranger,'' she continued. ''We've shared special moments.''

Pulling back gently to study her, he curved a finger under her chin, raising it for the kiss that was too long in coming. ''We'll have more. Many more.''

''Are you in there, Rafferty?'' a crackly voice asked outside the camper window.

Go away, Gaby wanted to scream, tightening her hold on the man in her arms.

''I'm here,'' Wyatt managed, breathing hard.

''We located cows on the other side of the wash,'' the man said. ''It's gonna take a bunch of us to cut 'em off. They're scared half to death.''

''I'll be there.''

''Wyatt,'' Gaby protested, holding onto him.

''I'll continue this later.'' He touched the tip of her nose with one finger. ''Count on it.''

She was sitting on the porch, still hoping Wyatt would drive in and keep his promise, when Frank ambled out to join her. He'd showered and smelled of a shaving lotion that was strong and outdoorsy. The sight of him, so like Wyatt, brought her a rush of pleasure.

Would she ever meet Pete? Was he cut from the same mold? Would the same touching vulnerability lie beneath the show of solid chin and chiseled Rafferty features?

Tomorrow she'd go to the cellar and bring the photo album upstairs where it should be. It would be exciting to study the faces of those Raffertys who lived before— those who had contributed to the stockpile of genes that resulted in the man she loved.

"What will Mr. and Mrs. Tierney do now?" she asked Frank.

"The house didn't sustain much damage. As for the barn, every able-bodied man in town will come by and see that the outbuildings get rebuilt."

"I've heard of people doing that." Gaby leaned on the rail, warmed by the thought of neighbor helping neighbor.

"But not where you come from?"

"It would be difficult for people to band together and rebuild a condo."

"I guess so." He put an arm around her and tightened his fingers briefly.

"With building codes and such it would be next to impossible," she said, feeling uncomfortable.

"That the first time you saw a fire?" His arm lowered to her waist.

"Up close," she said lightly, trying not to read too much into his action. Tonight had been difficult. He might be living through the aftereffects of danger.

"Never chased a fire truck when you were a kid?" he asked.

"No."

"Bet you were a spitfire, though." His fingers pressed and relaxed, pressed and relaxed.

"Where's Marianne?"

"She went to bed. I can't sleep. Too much excitement for me."

The sky was almost black now. There were no stars and the moon was in hiding. The smell of smoke was all that remained of the near tragedy.

"Mrs. Tierney said the hay caught fire by itself. How can that happen?" Gaby didn't hear his answer. She was too busy deciding what to say before she made a strategic withdrawal.

"Wyatt got a hero's welcome from you back at the fire," he said, after a long silence. "My knee got pretty banged up, too."

"You were both courageous."

A corner of his mouth twitched. "Is that all you've got to say about my injury?"

Gaby was losing her patience. "I assume it'll heal."

"But do you care?" He planted a kiss in her hair.

She brushed him away. "Please don't do that."

"You've been listening to gossip. I didn't think you were the upright, uptight type." His voice had an unattractive wheedling sound.

"You thought wrong. I am."

"Hey, this is your buddy, remember? You and I have secrets."

"Be my buddy at a distance, Frank," she said stiffly. "You're married. Marianne could get the wrong idea."

"Marianne isn't here."

"Oh, yes she is." Gaby moved a hand up and down between them meaningfully. "She's standing right here between us. Don't you realize how lucky you are?"

With a sigh of impatience, he clapped a hand to the back of his neck. "No lectures, teacher, that's why I quit school in the eleventh grade."

"Did you?"

"Yeah, but Pa made me go back."

"Good for him."

"Saving yourself for my brother?" he growled.

"Wyatt has nothing to do with this."

"You know he's going to end up with Ruthie, don't you? Where do you think they are now?"

"I wouldn't venture a guess."

"Don't bother guessing. It's a sure thing. They go way back."

"So I've been told."

"Won't do you any good to wait up for him. If they're still chasing down those cows, which I doubt, they'll make up for lost time before he comes home." His laugh rumbled deep in his chest.

His arm went around her again, and again she brushed him away, more strongly this time, the truth of what he'd said adding to her irritation. "Try that charm on your wife."

He looked genuinely hurt. "I love Marianne."

"I know you do, Frank," she said, searching his eyes with hers. "But I'm not sure she does." With that she went into the house, doing her best to chalk up his comments about Wyatt and Ruth Ann to jealousy.

Chapter Eleven

It was daylight before Wyatt returned, looking so worn Gaby was ashamed for listening to Frank's insinuations about his whereabouts. Volunteers had successfully rounded up all the strays, he said, and had arranged temporary housing until the barn could be rebuilt. Now he needed to catch a few hours' sleep.

The hours passed slowly. Gaby was disappointed, but went to work with a happy heart. There'd be time for them later, and it would be worth the wait.

Dinner tonight would be a celebration, she decided. Celebration of the Rafferty men's safety, of course, but privately, for Wyatt and herself. It would be a celebration of their discovery of each other as well.

In honor of the occasion, she took her time soaking in a warm bath, then donned her favorite dress—a peach linen shift, set off with a necklace of jasper and agate stones. She was putting on lip gloss, thinking of Wyatt kissing it off, when she heard angry voices. Though family bickering wasn't unknown under the Rafferty roof, she'd never heard shouting like this since her arrival.

Troubled, she inched her door open, just as Beau

backed out of the office, holding one hand in front of him. His face was scarlet.

"When I'm eighteen, I'm outta here!" he shouted.

"You won't get far on your own," Wyatt said, following him into the hall.

"Don't worry about me. I'll do just fine. I'll get a scholarship."

Carefully, Gaby eased the door closed again and stood with her back against it.

"You think it's that easy?" Wyatt asked.

"Gaby says I can. She says I have talent."

"And Gaby has all the answers?"

"She knows more than you do about it. I've been reading the stuff she gave me, and I won't need you or Dad holding my hand."

"Right now you aren't going anywhere." This time it was Frank speaking. "We're about to eat."

"You mean, *you're* about to eat. I'm leaving. What do you care? What do any of you care what happens to me? All that matters is that I work my fool neck off."

"Beau, come back here."

The front door slammed. Seconds later the pickup truck backed noisily out of the driveway and roared down the road.

"What's got into that boy?" Frank's words were muffled as he moved to the kitchen.

Gaby stayed in her room as long as she dared, wanting to give the family privacy while they discussed this new problem. But Marianne would need help with the meal. At the table, should she remark casually on what had happened, or pretend she hadn't heard?

Though she hadn't expected to see him, Wyatt was waiting for her in the hall. He'd dressed hurriedly in faded jeans and a white shirt, left unbuttoned over a T-shirt. Bluish circles under his eyes said he was still tired, though he'd evidently recovered enough from the previous night's ordeal to pounce on her.

"Had to mix in it, didn't you?" His voice was low but menacing.

"It isn't my fault if Beau wants more out of life than milking cows," she said, outraged at his accusation.

"More, is it?" He verbally underlined the word "more."

"I meant *different*."

"I heard you the first time."

"Don't take this out on me. I'm an innocent bystander."

"A bystander, yes. Innocent? No."

"I'm Mata Hari because I gave him a handful of brochures? Are you saying I'm to blame for what happened?"

His laugh was a snarl. "Aren't you?"

"Because your nephew has a mind of his own?"

"I don't intend to argue with you about this."

"Because you're endowed with a paranormal insight that tells you what's best for everybody else?"

"Back off, Gaby," he warned.

"Why?" A thought struck and she narrowed one eye. "Are you truly angry about my influence on Beau, or is it more?"

He snorted. "Meaning what?"

"Are you jumping on me because you're having regrets about what happened between us in the camper?"

He looked over his shoulder as if he thought someone might overhear. "I told you to back off. This isn't the time."

She considered his request but discarded it. "Are you only using Beau as an excuse to push me away? If so, you needn't bother. Neither of us was thinking clearly last night after the fire. I won't hold it against you."

"I'm telling you for the last time, Gaby," he said too calmly, not bothering to deny or affirm her suggestion. "Keep out of family business."

An ugly "or else" hung in the air between them for long moments until he turned away.

"What do you think Beau will do?" Marianne was saying as Gaby forced herself to join the family in the kitchen.

"He'll be all right," Frank assured her. "He lost his temper. It happens."

"Beau's not like that."

"All kids are like that sometimes."

Suppressing a sigh, Gaby arranged utensils at each place, including Beau's. At any minute, the boy would rethink what he'd said and come back. She'd try not to take Wyatt's accusations personally.

He resented—maybe even hated—her because of past experience. It would be so with anybody who came to Rafferty Farms from the city. She'd been a fool to think she could leap such a hurdle in their relationship so quickly. The key word was "patience."

The call came as they sat at the table and wordlessly began passing serving dishes. Frank leaned back, tipping his chair to get the phone. All color drained from his face as he listened. When he put the receiver down, he did it so quickly it missed the hook and dangled on its cord.

"That was Ruth Ann," he said. "A pickup truck full of teenagers took the Curve too fast. It crashed into the guardrail."

Marianne pressed both hands to her mouth. "Was it our truck? Was Beau in it?"

Frank ran his tongue over his lower lip. "I don't know. She just got the report and didn't have any details. The rescue squad is on its way to the scene."

"It can't be Beau," Gaby reminded them, trying not to sound worried. "He was alone."

"That doesn't mean he stayed alone," Wyatt shot back. "He probably picked up friends, looking for sympathy."

Marianne squeezed her husband's hand and pushed him toward the door. "Go, go, go, both of you. I'll stay in case he comes back."

"Right." Frank tore his jacket off the hook. "Honey, try not to worry. Beau's a careful driver."

"Usually. But he was upset when he left. There's no telling what he might have done. And there's his wrist. He shouldn't be driving at all."

Wyatt threw on a jacket, too, and joined his brother at the door. "We'll call the minute we know something."

"Yes, yes. Hurry."

When they were alone, Marianne looked at the table as if she didn't know how the food got there, then walked to the window, where she stood leaning heavily on her crutch. "This wouldn't have happened if . . ."

If Gaby hadn't come to Rafferty Farms?

"Should I clear the table?" Gaby asked, needing to do something.

"Leave it. If Beau comes home—I mean, *when* he comes home, he'll be hungry."

"Should we call his friends?"

"And tie up the phone lines?"

The minutes dragged by, a painful second at a time, with Gaby looking at the clock again and again, surprised to see that the hands had moved so little. The patter of Legs's paws sounded loud on the linoleum. The dog whined, as if he knew something was wrong, and rested his head on Gaby's leg.

When the phone finally rang, she started to it, but Marianne was there first, almost tripping over the cord in her haste. She listened only a few seconds before gasping in relief. "Oh, Frank, Frank. Thank goodness."

"It wasn't Beau?" Gaby asked.

Tears filled the woman's eyes and she shook her head. "Are the kids all right?" she asked. "I'm sorry. So sorry. If you can do anything to help, stay there. We can eat anytime. . . . No, I haven't heard from Beau. But he should be back any minute. . . . Fine. I'll see you soon."

Shortly after nine o'clock, Frank and Wyatt returned with news that the driver of the car, a boy who'd worked for the Rafferty family the previous summer, was still in critical condition. The other young passengers, only bruised and shaken, had been released to their parents' custody.

Beau came home after the dishes had been washed and put away. Neither he nor Marianne said anything about the earlier argument. She only pointed him to the leftovers in the fridge and told him to clean up after himself.

"I don't want to find pans soaking in the morning, or spills on the sink," she said, her voice uncharacteristically soft.

It was all over. She and Wyatt had blown up at each other before, Gaby reminded herself. This new trouble would pass the way everything else had.

She was wrong.

* * *

As she was finishing milkroom duty the next morning, Wyatt came in and asked the other workers to take a break. When they'd gone, he leaned a hand against the door to prevent Gaby from leaving, too.

"I called the old man this morning," he said. "Everything's arranged."

Her heart began to thump out of rhythm. "What old man is that?"

"Arnold Coburn. I told him you're doing a great job, but we aren't short of help anymore. An extra hand is only in the way."

"In other words, you lied." She concentrated on breathing evenly.

"Not so," he countered coldly. "You *are* in the way. He's satisfied that you fulfilled your obligation. You're to call him when you get back to the city."

"I see."

"I thought you'd be dancing on the ceiling. Here's the pardon you expected. Pack your suitcases and make whatever calls you need to get a ticket back where you came from."

"With Marianne still unable to pitch in, you need me."

"That isn't your worry. No hard feelings, Gaby. But you brought chaos with you. I expected it."

"Because Rolly did?"

He waited a minute before he continued. "For the peace of mind of everybody, we need you gone."

"You mean *you* need me gone."

"Put it any way you like. Go back to your beach. Lie in the sun and get the benefit of that light therapy." A smile came and went. "We never did get around to fixing your bed so it set north-south, did we?"

"Go back to my beach," she fumed. Determined to have the last word this time, she followed him into the yard and grabbed his arm. "Not everybody in Hollywood, California, is a movie star, Wyatt."

He raised an eyebrow. "Granted."

Sitting on a bench outside the milkroom, June and Bridget had their heads together. Both were listening to the exchange with undisguised interest.

"Not everybody who lives in Washington, D.C., is a senator."

"So?"

"So ordinary, everyday people live in Florida. People who don't own surfboards and never go to the beach. People who fight freeway traffic, go to offices, and raise families. People who attend church on Sundays and eat hot dogs at baseball games."

"What's your point?"

"I like it here."

"You haven't seen a Vermont winter."

She shook her head. "If I stirred things up, I'm glad. After that close call, I heard Marianne telling Frank that Beau can be an astronaut or a deep-sea diver if that's what he wants."

"Congratulations."

"So if Beau works hard, he'll be leaving after he

graduates, unless you make him feel so guilty he has to stay. Then you'll lose him entirely.''

''You know I wouldn't do that.''

''I don't know anything about you,'' she said. ''I thought I did.''

''I thought I knew you, too. We were both wrong.''

Sensing unrest, Legs trotted over and rubbed against Gaby's ankle. She reached down to scratch his head, for what would likely be the last time. She was going home. She'd never have to milk another cow or unclog another blower. She'd never have to drive another tractor, and best of all, face another of Wyatt's black scowls.

At the same time, her lips would never touch his. She'd never experience that spark of electricity she felt when he came in a room, or know the joy of hearing his voice.

''If you send me packing, who's going to do my job?'' she asked, wondering if his thoughts were anything like hers.

''We'll find somebody who knows how a farm works.''

''I know how a farm works.''

''Somebody who doesn't . . .''

''Make you crazy?'' she interrupted, hurling his words back at him.

''Meanwhile, Ruth Ann has offered to fill in.''

He'd already spoken to Ruth Ann? "She doesn't make you crazy?"

He raised his eyebrows in surprise. "She's a kid."

"She *was* a kid. Have you looked at her lately?"

"A few curves in the right places doesn't make a little girl a woman."

"So you've noticed?"

"I'm not dead." He crossed his arms over his chest. "Now will you go, and let me get back to work? I appreciate your help, Gaby. It isn't your fault that you don't fit in. You even have Frank and Marianne fighting. That's something they never did before."

"How did I accomplish that?"

"A word here, a word there. This morning she gave him an ultimatum."

"If it's about his roving eye, good for her." Gaby folded her arms, too, aping his stance. "Surely you can't be on his side in that?"

"Do you hear yourself? 'His side? Her side?' " Wyatt questioned. "Before you showed up on the doorstep nobody had to take sides about anything."

"Then I did something right." What was the use? She was fighting an uphill battle. "Okay. I tried." She started away but came back.

"Forget something?"

"Just this. Do you know why you like cows so much? Because they gaze at you with velvety brown eyes full of unquestioning love, and you can lead them around by a rope.''

If he was ruffled by her comment, it didn't show. His face was as expressionless as a mask. ''Tell me what time your bus leaves,'' he said coldly. ''One of us can take you to the station.''

Chapter Twelve

"It's so sudden." Marianne had tears in her eyes. "You were getting to be one of us."

Wyatt hadn't told the rest of the family the reason for Gaby's sudden departure. She'd had to elaborate on the opportunity she couldn't afford to ignore at Lennox Ink. Worse, he didn't bother to put in an appearance to say good-bye. She could hear him in the distance going at the fallen oak with his chain saw.

"I know," she said. "But you don't need me anymore. Before long you'll be dancing on the rooftops."

"Bite your tongue." Marianne laughed. "Are you sure I can't convince you to stay?"

"My career calls."

"Don't forget your poster," Beau reminded her. "And your calendar."

"I think I'll leave them, if you don't mind," she said, knowing she'd feel hurt all over again by sight of the big black X's she'd once made on the calendar, marking off her days of confinement. "No more room in my suitcase. I bought too many souvenirs."

"Souvenirs of Woodbridge?" Beau scoffed.

"Let us hear from you," Marianne said. "Don't be a stranger."

Gaby nodded her agreement, though she had no intention of calling or writing. A sharp break with Rafferty Farms would be her only chance to pick up the threads of her life again.

"Ready, Sunshine?" Frank asked, when he'd stowed her bags in the back of the pickup.

On and on the saw sounded in the distance, and she caught her lower lip between her teeth. "All ready."

"Thought you were unsinkable," Frank said when they were on their way to the bus stop.

"I thought I was, too."

"It isn't me, is it?" His eyes were Wyatt's eyes. Gray-green in the morning light and shadowed with concern. "If I stepped out of line, I'm sorry."

"It isn't you, Frank," she said truthfully.

In spite of his problems, lesser now, she hoped, due to Marianne's standing up for herself, she liked him. He'd helped her through a time when she'd needed a friend badly.

The bus was late, but unlike the bus in her dreams, it stopped. She got on, took a window seat, and opened a crossword puzzle magazine she'd bought at the Country Store. Setting to work with a Number 2 pencil, she concentrated on not looking out the window. Glimpses of passing scenery—spotted cows, pastures, and neatly squared-off farmland—would only make her sad as she realized she was no longer part of it.

They reached the first rest stop an hour later, but she decided not to get off when the others did. This wasn't an express bus and they'd be making many such stops.

She was well into the second puzzle's solution when her fellow passengers began to file back in again. All she needed to finish was an eleven-letter word for "sorcerer." Trying not to be distracted by a rumble of conversation between the driver and another passenger, she tapped a finger on the page.

"Magician." No. That was only eight letters.

"Which one is she?" the driver asked.

"The one in the blue coat."

The voice arrowed its way through her concentration, and she looked up, not able to believe anyone else had Wyatt's voice.

No one did. Wyatt had one foot in the stairwell and the other on the sidewalk. His hair was shaggy, as if he hadn't taken time to comb it, and he was still wearing the Paul Bunyan coat. The other passengers were in their seats, waiting. A head count had been made.

"Miss, this guy says he has to talk to you," the driver called. "He says you should get off."

"Not a chance." Digging her fingernails into the palms of her hands, Gaby fastened her gaze out the window, where a grim-faced woman in a knit hat was waiting for the bus to pull out so she could cross the street.

"He says it's an emergency," the driver said.

"I paid for a ticket and I'm staying where I am."

"She says she's not going," the driver grunted, as if Wyatt needed an interpreter. "Step down, sir. We have a schedule to keep."

"You know all about schedules, don't you, Wyatt?" Gaby threw at him. "Let this man keep his."

"I don't want you to go," Wyatt said.

"That isn't what you said two hours ago."

"I didn't know how impossible it would be not having you around."

"One of you has to get off," the driver insisted. "Now."

"Where's your next stop?" Wyatt asked him.

"Stonehurst. Why do you want to know?"

"Gaby." Wyatt looked back at her again. "Ride in the car with me as far as Stonehurst and we can talk. If you still want to go, you can reboard the bus. I won't try to stop you."

"Go with him, honey," said the heavyset woman in the seat next to Gaby, jabbing her in the ribs with an elbow. "He looks like a sweet young man."

"Looks can be deceiving."

"Please, Gaby," Wyatt tried.

"Mister, you'd better go before I lose my temper." The driver's voice rose an octave with his impatience.

"Gaby, I need you." Wyatt had stepped into the bus and was lumbering down the aisle toward her.

"Right. You need me to milk the cows."

"No. I need you—because I need you."

"Why?"

"Because I love you." He looked back at the driver. "Could I trouble you to unlock the luggage compartment? I'll take her suitcases off."

"Leave them." Gaby thrust out a restraining hand. "I've seen the last I want to see of Vermont, Mr. Rafferty. And the worst is yet to come. Your winters are killers."

"I'll keep you warm," Wyatt promised.

"Awww." The heavyset woman jabbed Gaby in the side again with her elbow.

"That's it," the driver growled, charging down the aisle too. "Off you go, mister, or I get security. You heard the lady."

"I'm sorry for the things I said to hurt you," Wyatt went on, not noticing that the man was tugging at his sleeve. "It was only because I was afraid. People destroy other people every day in the name of love."

"I know." It was exactly what she'd told herself when she arrived and made a resolution to get close to no one.

"That's why I kept pushing you away. I thought I'd get to where I couldn't do without you, and you'd leave."

She blinked back tears. "You don't think that anymore?"

He shook his head. "It's too late to worry about it. The damage is done."

"Damage? Not a particularly romantic choice of words."

"I only meant that I can't do without you, Gaby. I'll have to cross my fingers and hope nothing happens to send you away from me."

"Nothing could possibly happen," she admitted, unable to steady her runaway heartbeat long enough to continue fighting. "I love you, too."

"Sometimes I believed you did. Other—"

"I know the feeling," she interrupted, grinning foolishly.

Wyatt grinned, too, and held out his arms. "Let's go."

"I'll drink to that." The bus driver sounded tired.

After they'd retrieved her luggage, they watched until the bus was out of sight, returning the waves of some of the other passengers. Cars passed, and pedestrians stepped around them, some clicking their tongues, making sounds of impatience. Gaby didn't care.

"It's still hard for me to believe," Wyatt said, holding her so close she could hardly get her breath, now and then dipping down to collect a kiss.

"What's hard to believe?"

"You're willing to trade in the beach, fancy shopping malls, and exotic restaurants for long johns, Deke's Odds and Ends, and a sack lunch next to the pond."

"No way." She tilted her head back. "I don't intend to give up anything."

"You don't?" One shaggy eyebrow raised quizzically.

"We have summer in Vermont, don't we?"

"A day or two."

"We aren't isolated from the world. A scenic drive will take us to Burlington. If we want to go farther, there are always buses, planes, and trains."

"True. But you're abandoning your dream."

She shook her head. "Like I said, I won't give anything up. I'll have my home office."

"What home office is that?"

"We can share space, can't we? I'm sure I can make arrangements, with whatever company hires me, to work out of the house and drive to the city only when necessary."

"Hires you?" he questioned.

"Hires me," she repeated.

"Excuse me, folks." A deliveryman pushing a dolly covered with boxes maneuvered his way around them.

"It sounds like you had this all figured out," Wyatt said, taking her elbow as they moved to one side.

"I put out a feeler or two when Marianne and I went to the city."

"Pretty sure of yourself, weren't you?" he accused.

"I was getting that way. Until you booted me out."

"Sorry about that. But you stepped off that bus looking like everything I'd ever dreamed of, and I began to understand why my brother went to New York."

A thought struck, and she looked at him squarely. "Hold on. When you came after me today, were you assuming that I'd agree to go on milking cows and making chocolate milk?"

"The truth?" He raised his shoulders and lowered them. "Actually, I was. But I understand your feelings."

"Wyatt, your cows know who's boss, and it's not me." She waited for her words to sink in. "You don't mind that I don't intend to work at the dairy anymore?"

"I can live with it," he said, after an interminable moment of contemplation. "Not everybody in Hollywood, California, is a movie star. Not everybody in Washington, D.C., is a congressman. And not everybody in Vermont milks cows."

"Naturally, I'll help out until you get someone to take my place."

"No need. I'll get Ruthie."

"Forget Ruthie." She fastened him with an adamant stare. "I said I'd help out."

A smile lit up his eyes. "Now that our peace talk is over, let's go home."

Home. It was the most beautiful word Gaby had ever heard.

"Marianne will be happy to see you," he went on as they walked across a square of grassy lawn to the parking lot. "She's the one who gave me the kick where it counts and sent me after you."

"I'm glad." Gaby had halfway suspected that the woman's friendly good-bye had been due partly to seeing the last of an unwelcome guest.

"Later we'll need a place of our own. You've noticed the cottage across the road from the restaurant?"

She nodded. "It belonged to Pete and Rolly."

"It'll be ours after we're married. You can make whatever changes you want to make. Curtains. Carpets. Colors."

Ours, she thought, experiencing a sense of exhilaration. At this point she wouldn't have cared if they had no curtains at all, and the walls were polka dots. "Any changes to be made, we'll make together."

When they reached the pickup truck, he gave his car keys a shake, and his old troubled expression returned. "If there's a chance you might change your mind and want to leave later, tell me now. I need to be prepared."

"Not getting cold feet, are you?" she teased.

"Not me. But you've seen how tight the schedule can be at the farm. Sometimes we may not find enough time for each other."

"You're wrong, Wyatt. We'll always find time." With a joyous sense of possession, she grasped his sleeves and pulled him down for the first kiss they would share that was entirely free of doubts. "I guarantee it."